LOVING HIS FLOWER SHOP GIRL

AN ENEMIES TO LOVERS ROMANCE

BRITNEY M MILLS

CRYSTAL CANYON PUBLISHING

CHAPTER 1

*B*ecca Taylor's morning wasn't going as planned. After waking up late, her hair wouldn't cooperate into the usual soft curls she liked. And there was almost nothing she could do for the puffiness under her eyes after a long night of nightmares.

As she heated her oatmeal in the microwave, Becca's mind glossed over the memories that kept recurring in her mind, the ones where she pictured her parents' and brother's deaths after sliding off a cliff in their car. The images that kept her bound to Sage Creek.

She'd been dressed in her graduation cap and gown, ready to receive the certificate for her bachelor's degree, and it was the moment her carefree and adventurous life had come to a halt. She knew it, and yet the ability to break away from her rigid routine was something she struggled with.

Control was the name of the game, and most days she conquered. But not today.

Glancing down at her blouse, she glared at the glob of warm oatmeal she'd just dropped that was now seeping through. Another outfit change was not what she had in mind. The clock told her she was already ten minutes late leaving the house. The thought of her tardiness caused that familiar knot to form in her stomach.

Since the accident, being late was something Becca hated. Her father, who'd grown up in a military family, had often wanted to strangle her as a teenager as she arrived when she was ready. But now, even five and a half years after his death, she remembered his words and stuck by them almost religiously.

The measure of a person is noted in their appreciation of time, especially the time of others.

She didn't necessarily have anyone waiting on her at the moment, as her flower shop opened in twenty minutes, but the fact was she was all about routine and order, not change. When that routine was thrown, it seemed as though everything went with it.

What if something life-threatening happened because she was late? It was the one thing she wished she could change about that day so long ago. That on the one day her parents had left late, they would've been able to avoid the car which had been speeding past, clipping the back bumper.

"It'll be all right, Becca," she tried to tell herself, pushing the thoughts from her mind.

She changed her shirt, opting for a short-sleeved one with a sweater over top. At least if she spilled again, she could remove the top layer. Her makeup would have to go on at the shop. She'd only see Karla, the town coffee shop owner, before then, and she could handle that.

Running outside, Becca lengthened her stride, passing her flower shop and coming to the corner of the street in seconds before turning south onto Main Street. She loved living next to the shop, making it easier to bring flowers from her garden out back into the back room once they were ready.

The fact that the coffee shop was only two units down from her place made it even sweeter. The benefit of living in a small town, as compared to the large city where she'd gone to college, was that most things were in walking distance.

She glanced back, breathing a sigh of relief as she didn't see many people walking along the street, until she hit something hard, knocking her backward and almost onto her backside.

As she felt the momentum take her one way, a warm hand caught her wrist, stopping her fall and pulling her back up and off her feet. With her head buried in the flannel shirt of her rescuer, Becca wondered if this day could get any worse.

Stepping back, she glanced up, arching her head more than normal. Sure, she was only five foot four, but she felt as if she was looking sky-high at the brown-haired, brown-eyed vision standing before her. Her heart thumped as her eyes focused even more, and the similarities between him and another man from her past sent the adrenaline rushing through her.

"I'm so sorry. It's been a morning." She glanced at her shoes, realizing that although both shoes were black, they were different patterns. Groaning inwardly, she looked back up, sweeping back a section of her hair. "Thank you for, um, saving me from total embarrassment."

She took a step to the side, hoping to continue her path around him. She didn't need to think about her ex-fiancé on top of everything that had already gone wrong today.

"Not a problem. Glad I could be of assistance, Miss—" He held out his hand, his eyebrows near his hairline.

She stopped, trying to be polite while guarding her heart from the memories that flashed in her mind. "Taylor. Becca Taylor. Who are you?"

He smiled, accentuating a scar on the side of his chin. "Colton Maxfield. I just arrived last night, but this little town seems…nice." The forced compliment caused Becca to frown. She'd had her fair share of people downing the small town over the years, and from that history, they didn't usually stick around long.

"Well, I hope we can convince you that we really are *nice*, Mr. Maxfield. It was nice to meet you, but I'm late." She nodded and skirted around the side of him, making a beeline for the coffee shop at the end of the block. As she walked in, the line stretched back to the door, and Becca ground her teeth together.

"Becca!" a voice called from behind the counter. Karla had spotted her and waved her forward. "What happened to you this morning? Your tea is probably cold by now." The older woman handed her a cup, and while it wasn't as steaming hot as usual, it was still quite warm.

"Thank you, Karla. Long night, and I slept in. But things are looking up now that I have this." Becca grinned as she lifted the cup a few inches. She took a sip, feeling some of the tension seep away. "You are a lifesaver. Remind me about this when you need flowers."

Karla chuckled and nodded. "Will do, girl. Better get going. I know how you are with your schedule."

Becca turned, waving to just about everyone in line as she moved past. She turned right once outside and walked back to her flower shop. Pulling out her key, she opened the door and breathed in the smell of the flowers, something that never seemed to grow old no matter how long she'd owned the store.

"Morning, Becca," Carissa said once Becca made it to the back room. She was a high school junior who'd been working at the shop for several months now. Having her there was fun because Becca got to be boss and teacher at the same time, and with how fast Carissa picked things up, it took some of the pressure off Becca.

"Good morning, Carissa. I didn't expect you in so early today." Becca dropped her things onto the large table next to the wall and pulled on an apron from the same area.

Carissa nodded. "It was one of those teacher prep days. I figured I'd come in since we have that big order coming up for the wedding this Saturday. Do you need me to order more lilies?"

Glancing over at the large cooler where most of the flowers were stored, Becca mentally went over the number of flowers they'd need. "I ordered a bunch to come in on Thursday, but it might be good to double-check so we aren't scrambling right before the wedding."

"Are you all right, Becca?" Carissa's eyebrows were scrunched together with concern.

Becca hadn't realized she was twisting her fingers together, causing the knuckles to turn white against her already pale skin.

"I'm fine. I just feel off today." She thought about the events of the morning again, and the picture of the handsome stranger popped into her mind. "Do you know a Colton Maxfield?"

Carissa put down the scissors as she picked up several already cut stems, placing them in a box. "I've heard of him. He got in last night and stayed at the hotel. Mom checked him in."

Carissa's mother, Delia, had owned and managed the hotel since her husband died two years earlier from cancer. The woman worked hard but was the source of gossip in the small town. She knew a lot of what was going to happen before it did, so of course she knew the new guy in town.

"How long is he here for?" Becca asked, trying to be casual. She didn't need people thinking she'd taken an interest in the stranger, because her heart was still locked up, not ready to attempt love again. The last thing she needed was the pity blind dates the women of this town could contrive at a moment's notice.

"I think quite a while. Mom said something about him working on that new development down the road. I guess they're putting in a bunch of townhomes and apartments?" Carissa leaned over the table, filling out the paper for the order she'd just boxed up, not really showing any emotion when it came to the development.

Becca felt enough for her anyway. She'd been elected to the city council the year before, and she loved every minute of the politics and helping make decisions that impacted the town. This was one decision that still hurt.

She and Richard Lawson were the only ones to vote against a preliminary meeting to look into the development, thinking that by bringing in the smaller housing on the south end of town, they would be changing the dynamic of the town. And if there was one thing Becca didn't like, it was change, of any sort. Change only brought heartache and a lack of control, the kind that lasted far after the events had taken place.

She thought back to the man on the street and realized she should have guessed he was some kind of builder. Her ex-fiancé had been one too, and while he typically wore suits to work, there was a certain confidence about contractors that she should have seen despite the flannel shirt Colton wore earlier.

Taking a few minutes to put on her makeup, Becca tried to get the image of the man out of her head. The commonalities between him and her ex-fiancé, just from a two-minute conversation, were throwing her brain for a loop. And if he was going to be staying in town for several weeks, how was she going to avoid him?

Shaking her head, she put her makeup bag back into her purse and focused on the list of orders that had come in at the end of yesterday. Sorting through the flowers that had been delivered that morning, she tried to find the ones she needed, all the while pushing thoughts of her past to the background. She hadn't had so many memories come to the surface in months, and it took several focused distractions to finally help the tension in her body ease up.

A few hours later, Becca walked into the main room of her flower shop, bringing two vases of tulips to sit in the front cooler. The store had been busy that morning but had slowed down for the afternoon rush. She'd dropped off the weekly orders around town and then came back to relieve Carissa, grateful for all she'd done to help get the orders ready before leaving for the day.

The break in customers was nice because as much as she loved flowers, holidays seemed to kick everything up a notch, even in the small town of Sage Creek. With the Founder's Day Festival two weeks away, she knew the two days before would be the most stressful of the year, trying to get all the flowers in, cut, and arranged.

She couldn't imagine living anywhere but this quaint town, nestled as it was in the mountains of western Colorado. She'd grown up in Sage Creek, only leaving to earn a degree. The minute she got to school in Salt Lake, she'd realized that there really was no place like home. The bustling city, while exhilarating and fun in many respects, now seemed tainted by the death of her family. Her small town provided just about everything she needed, and things were predictable, helping to keep her anxiety to a minimum.

After the three and a half years it took to get a bachelor's degree in interior design, her plan had been to stay in the city, interning for a popular designer. But the safe haven of Sage Creek had been the balm to her soul once she'd been able to stop the tears from falling. She'd opened up her flower shop and decided this was where she'd stay. A place of low crime and low risk made life bearable.

The doorbell chimed, and she looked up with a ready smile to see the mayor walk in.

"Mayor Watkins. What a surprise. Was there something wrong with this week's order? I just dropped it by Town Hall a couple of hours ago." She closed the door to the storage case and rested her hands on her hips.

The old man chuckled. "No, nothing was wrong. The women have all been ogling it. I'm actually here on personal business." He grimaced. "I need something for Dottie. I forgot that it's our half-something today, and I'm already in trouble for forgetting."

Becca grinned. "Half what?"

"I'm not really sure. That woman keeps track of every date and every first of everything, which is why I'm in the doghouse most of the time. I figured some flowers would smooth it over." He rolled his eyes and shook his head as he smiled, causing Becca to laugh.

A picture of the mayor's wife popped into her head. For the most part, Becca expected people with white hair to be sweet and full of wisdom. Dorothy Watkins could be just that at times, but she was a firecracker for the most part, and it was easier to stay on her good side rather than to have to win her back over. But then again, she and the mayor had been married over forty years now, having celebrated the mile-stone the year before in a big town party. The two of them were like surrogate grandparents, and she was grateful for all they did for her.

"A couple of lilies, then? I know they're her favorite."

The mayor pointed at her. "See, this is why I come to you. You know just about everything about everyone in this town, especially their favorite flowers. Can you wrap them in some paper so I can take them?"

"Of course. Let me run back and get some for you." Becca strode into the back room and pulled some fresh lilies from the cooler. She didn't want Mrs. Watkins to have anything to complain about, even a small brown spot on a petal. If there was one good source of free advertising for Becca in this town, it was the fact that when Mayor Watkins bought his wife flowers, she told the world.

Not that Becca had any competition, being the only flower place around, but it was still nice to nudge people her way. When the townspeople's budgets grew tighter, money for flowers was put on hold, and she appreciated all the business she could get from this small town.

Resuming her spot out front, she rolled the few flowers in some tissue paper and tied them with a pink ribbon. Typing the figures into the cash register, she looked up and asked, "Cash or card?"

"Cash." He handed her a twenty-dollar bill. "I'll get these home before the council meeting tonight. You'll be there, right?"

"I wouldn't miss it. I hear we've got some interesting items on the agenda." She raised her eyebrows and grinned. Again, the handsome stranger popped into her mind, causing her to wonder what was wrong with her brain and its fixation with the builder.

"Yeah. That new subdivision has caused quite the ruckus. But we'll figure it out, right? That's what we always do in this town. We may argue for a little bit, but when we make a decision, we put the past behind us."

"That right there is one of the reasons I'm still here, Mayor. Putting the past behind us and moving on." Several different thoughts clouded her mind at once, and she had to push them away, focusing on the present before her. "I'll see you tonight."

She handed him the bouquet of flowers and went back to

cleaning up, her thoughts drifting to how building would impact the town.

The mayor had talked her ear off about the subdivision two nights before when Dorothy had invited her over for dinner. He was in favor of the growth, but for all of the reasons he thought it would be good, Becca just shook her head and hoped it wouldn't go through.

The contractor was trying to build thirty homes, along with several apartment buildings. Although it wouldn't double the population of the town, it would significantly impact it. The thought of outsiders—people who didn't share the same vision as the people of Sage Creek—disrupting the dynamic made Becca worry.

Tonight's weekly Wednesday meeting would be interesting, that was for sure. It wasn't some big theater production or sporting event, but sometimes she was tempted to bring a bag of popcorn and watch as the petty drama unfolded. Peter would've laughed at that thought, because what excited him were city lights and thousands of people. Something she should have noticed long before he disappeared.

Shaking her head, Becca pushed thoughts of her ex-fiancé away, knowing she had to forget about him at some point. She'd worry about the forever later and hope that the small things would take over the ache she still felt from their breakup a year and a half before.

CHAPTER 2

olton Maxfield pulled out the three sets of plans he'd been given before he came out to this small town. He was used to working in Denver where everything was loud, busy, and crowded. After arriving in Sage Creek the night before, he hadn't slept well. How did people actually sleep when the night was so silent?

He'd thought about getting up in the middle of the night to research those sound machines, but once the fan kicked on, it seemed to do the trick, lulling him to sleep. It had been so long since he'd been in a quiet town, but even where he'd grown up had been somewhat close to the railway station, meaning train whistles and sounds going off at random times during the night.

His time in Sage Creek depended on the outcome of the town council's preliminary meeting that night. He would deliver the plans and answer any questions the people had. After that, and some due diligence, he'd hopefully be able to drive back to Denver with a letter of approval to build. That was the biggest test, if he could persuade the people of this town that a little growth would only benefit them, not take away their livelihood.

Adam Summers, his boss, had already warned him that the town might not be friendly about the development, and Colton was preparing to win them over, going over different scenarios while waiting for the day to pass.

The coffee shop in the middle of town had been the perfect place to study the plans, better than the stuffy room at the hotel. He had to make sure he knew them inside and out because there was nothing worse than not having an answer for something important, which usually caused his mind to go blank. He'd felt like an idiot on more than one occasion, and if he could prep himself to avoid it, that's what he did.

The woman who'd bumped into him that morning kept coming to mind, and while Colton wasn't in the market for love, something about her caused his curiosity to roar to life. He'd always loved people-watching, from the time he was little at the playground until now, where he'd analyze people as they passed him on the street. It was one of the reasons Adam had sent him here, to make sure he read the reactions and smoothed things over.

But there was something about that woman, her dark brown hair draped over her shoulders and those hazel eyes boring right through him. She'd thrown him off for a few seconds, but he was glad he'd somewhat regained his composure. Not that any woman would be interested in a long-term relationship with a guy who'd barely graduated high school. He'd gone through a fair amount of rejection from his lack of impressive resume.

Since the coffee shop didn't offer anything but muffins and scones to eat, Colton had walked to a diner for a late lunch. As he continued to prepare through the afternoon, his brain was nearing the mush stage. He'd been focusing on all the details for much longer than he was used to.

Being a project manager would definitely stretch him, if he actually landed the job. He was used to the mindless measuring and cutting of boards and nailing them onto walls, working for hours in this manner. But having to prep for negotiating an entire subdivision seemed to be like prepping for a pop quiz. All the information left as soon as he tried to recall it a few minutes later.

Soon, the clock on the wall said ten to seven. He'd better get over to the town hall. Nothing was worse than being late to convince people of growth.

Colton hopped into his two-year-old Chevy and turned on the ignition. He still sighed at the roar of the diesel engine. It was a company truck, but Colton treated it like his baby. As he drove down the road several blocks, he remembered his old 90s Toyota with mismatched paint. He'd had to wiggle the key in the ignition every time, hoping it would start for him. And on the colder days, well, he arrived at places looking more like a popsicle than a working man.

Pulling into the parking lot around back of Town Hall on the north end of town, he saw several cars already parked. A few people walked through the back door, while others stood just outside. Adrenaline shifted through him. He hoped it would just be the city council since it was a preliminary meeting. He always felt a lot of pressure when addressing a big group, but with smaller numbers, it was easier for Colton to relax and answer questions.

Walking into the air-conditioned building, a woman looked him up and down and said in an overly sweet voice, "May I help you?"

"Yeah, I'm, uh, here for the meeting?" Colton scrunched his face, hoping to make the woman laugh. Instead, she seemed more intent on staring at him. The seconds ticked by, and Colton was afraid to move a muscle, watching as she eyed him up and down.

He gulped, hoping she'd give him the directions soon enough. He wasn't good at being ogled, and he could see the wheels turning in her head. Not that he'd dated that many women in his life, but he knew that look, the one that told him they were contemplating something clever to catch his interest, which usually didn't work.

"I'm Susie Jones. I don't work here, but most of the meetings are held down at the end of the building." She turned and pointed down the hall, smiling at him again.

Colton jumped. "Uh, thank you." He took several steps away, getting the sense he needed to keep his guard up when around her in the future.

Hearing a few voices, he moved in that direction. As he walked into the room, he saw at least twenty people. A large table was set up with seven people sitting around it while a handful of other people sat in folding chairs throughout the room. Taking a seat at the back, Colton looked around, noting small details of all the people around him. Anything that could help him through this meeting.

An older man at the table yelled for quiet, his strained voice calling the room to order. "We'd like to welcome you all out to this week's town council meeting. We'll be hearing from some of our townsfolk first before we move through the agenda. I think Agnes had something to discuss?"

A woman stood up two rows in front of Colton, her back toward him. "Yeah, I'm here to complain about Farmer Henson's dog. It's kept me up the last few nights. I know he is basically a member of their family, but there's got to be something we can do so the dog isn't waking up the whole neighborhood."

Colton rested his head on the wall behind him. He hoped this would go fast. With all that needed to be accomplished on this trip, he didn't have time to listen to every moment of bickering the people in town had. He went over the questions the council would ask him, feeling pretty good about the answers he gave, even if only in his mind.

Almost dozing off, he was grateful when the mayor finally said, "Complaints are over. It's time to begin with what we've got set up on the agenda tonight. If you don't want to stay, feel free to leave now. Otherwise, let us begin. Becca, what's the first thing we need to discuss?"

Colton's head popped up, surprised to hear her name. It was the same woman from that morning, only this time, she was wearing black-rimmed spectacles. Colton studied her, squinting so he could see clearer. She was striking, giving him a girl-next-door vibe. As she spoke, he could see an air of confidence and knowledge that impressed him.

"We've received several complaints that the levee is getting weak in some spots. We need to hire someone to get those fixed, even though it's late in the rain season." She glanced around the table, looking at the men and women around her.

Colton grinned, grateful she wasn't looking in his direction. She seemed to be a firecracker, which was probably something this town needed.

One of the guys across the table from her spoke, and Colton crossed his fingers, hoping it wouldn't take forever for them to get to his subdivision on the agenda. The man's answer was quick, and the Becca woman finally said, "Sunnyside Farm Subdivision." She took off her glasses and chewed on the end, her almond eyes more visible now, drawing out the color in her cheeks.

Remembering that Sunnyside was his reason for being

there, Colton stood. "I'm here to represent Dream Homes Inc." He stepped forward, setting the roll of plans on the council table.

The older man who had called the room to order looked at Colton, his eyes narrowed as he searched Colton's face. "Welcome to Sage Creek. What's your name, son?"

"Colton Maxfield, sir." Colton shifted his weight to the side, feeling uncomfortable under the scrutiny of all the eyes on him.

"It's nice to meet you. I'm Mayor Watkins, and we have our financial planner here to my left, Darcy Sunbolt. Next to her is the recreational manager, Jacob Downey. Richard Lawson is down there at the end. Across the table is Stacy Goodfellow, David Wallaby, and Becca Taylor. What position do you hold in the company?"

It took a minute for him to register all the names and then another minute for him to realize they were waiting for him to speak.

"Fini— I mean, project manager, sir."

"Where you from, Colton?" the mayor asked.

It wasn't his favorite question because his family had bounced around as a kid. "All over, mostly Boulder, but I've lived in Denver for the past twelve years."

"Well, we're glad you could come out and see the beauty that is Sage Creek. Now, talk to us. What is it that Dream Homes has proposed for our little town?" The man sat back with his hands on his stomach, one eyebrow raised.

It was finally showtime. Colton just hoped his brain would cooperate. He could feel Becca's eyes on him, the set of her mouth revealing she wasn't in favor of this proposal.

"Those plans," he said, motioning to the stack of papers on the table, "are for the new subdivision on the south end of Sage Creek. My boss has done quite a bit of research, with surveying and groundwater tests, to make sure this would be a benefit for your town."

Becca turned her eyes on him, pulling the glasses away from her mouth long enough to say, "What if we don't think we need new houses and apartment buildings?"

Colton tried to hide his smile at having correctly assessed her opinion with just a few seconds of studying her body language. She was attractive, but with an attitude like that, he'd have more fun rolling around with the pigs he'd seen on one of the farms a few streets over. But this was one of the scenarios he'd rehearsed, and with his shoulders back, he felt a surge of confidence flow through him.

"From the numbers I've seen, the population of Sage Creek is on the decline. New structures and apartment buildings will allow families who want to take part in the small-town experience to do so. This will help keep your town thriving through the years." Colton returned her stare, but her expression revealed nothing.

"What did the groundwater tests say? And would the water pressure decrease throughout the town from the number of new builds?" The questions came from the man named Jacob. If he was the rec manager, he was probably worried about the state of the grounds he managed.

Colton sorted through some of the papers he'd kept with him, hoping he'd brought those papers with him. After going through each paper individually, his stomach sank.

"It looks like I left the documentation back at the hotel. Groundwater tests came back normal, and from everything I've read, there is enough water in the town to sustain the buildings we're proposing. I can make sure copies are given to each of you by morning so you can see for yourselves." Colton could kick himself for not remembering to bring all the documents. He just hoped they could see he was being honest and not trying to manipulate the vote.

"That would be great, Colton. I appreciate your time coming here with these plans for us," the mayor said. "We'll need a few days to look at them, and then we can ask more questions and vote on how we'll proceed from here."

"We can vote now. I'm not sure a few days could ever sway us toward going through with this project." Becca's voice sounded like acid, and it caused Colton to wonder what she didn't like about the whole project.

The mayor held up a hand and said, "This is a big decision for the town, and as its governing members, we need to make sure we make the right decision. Everything Colton said is true. This will help some newer and younger families to come in and be a part of our community."

A man at the end of the table spoke, his face etched with frustration. "I've lived here since I was born, and so have my father and my grandfather and my great-grandfather. We've been in this town long enough to know that with a bunch of outsiders, the dynamic of our town will change completely. I don't think a subdivision is a good idea. In fact, it could be the division that makes the town fall. Why can't we just leave it how it is now? With only the current members of the community living here?"

Colton had never heard such elitism, and here they were in the twenty-first century.

The mayor opened his mouth, his lips barely moving as he said, "Thank you, David. We—"

"A lot of us come from original Sage Creek stock, but that doesn't mean we can't welcome others into our midst. Some people are just looking for a grand opportunity to get out of the city, and why not make it easy enough for them to find their dream home in our quaint little town?" one of the women said.

Colton felt a little more at ease, knowing he wasn't going

to have to go against the entire committee to get this passed. His boss wouldn't be happy if Colton didn't get the plans approved in the next week or two. He just hoped he didn't have to stick around here for that long.

The mayor spoke up again. "Okay, we'll meet again next Wednesday to discuss the options and come to a decision on the subdivision project. Becca, is there anything else we need to discuss for this meeting?"

The woman looked down at the paper in front of her and shook her head.

"Okay, then we'll dismiss for the evening."

"So we'll make the final decision on it at our next meeting?" Becca said with her pen poised over the paper. She must be the secretary.

"Yes. I'd also like each of us to visit the site to make sure we think of all the ins and outs that allowing this to go forward will impact."

Colton groaned. A week? What was he going to do around here for a week? The town didn't even have a movie theater, let alone any regular restaurants. His stomach gurgled with the greasy fries stuck to the bottom of it. His room had a little hot plate and a few dishes and pots. He'd have to plan out what he'd cook, pretending as if he were at home. Otherwise, he was going to be in pain over the next few days from all the eating out.

The meeting adjourned, and Colton went back to his seat to pick up his phone and other files from the seat next to where he'd been sitting. As he stood to turn around, Becca slammed into him and went flying backward, papers flying in every direction around them.

She looked up at him and frowned, opening her mouth as if she were ready to rip him apart. But then her mouth closed, and Colton wasn't sure what she was trying to say.

He reached out his hand toward her. "I'm so sorry. I really didn't mean to run into you...again."

Avoiding his hand, she pushed off the ground and moved around, collecting pieces of paper and stuffing them back into a folder. Could she be any more obnoxious?

Getting all the paperwork resettled, she pushed past him with a scowl and walked out of the building. The other council members filed past, not saying much as they left the room.

When the mayor passed by, he said, "I see you met Becca face to face?" The grin on his face confused Colton.

"Yeah, I don't think she's too fond of me at the moment." Colton turned to look at the empty doorway as if Becca would storm back in to agree with him. The mayor's voice caused him to turn back.

"Well, if you really want this subdivision to go through, you might want to start working on her."

"Excuse me?" Colton leaned a little closer, not sure he'd heard the man correctly.

"I'm saying, if you want to take a signed paper to your boss saying that you're good to build the proposed homes and apartments, you need to find a way to get that girl on your side."

With a frown, Colton said, "Aren't you the mayor? Isn't that why they elected you? To make the best decision for the town?"

"I also don't get a vote in this process, and you'll need a majority vote here. Becca has an incredible way of persuading people, and this town turns to her for a lot. She's kind of the town darling. People have looked out for her for several years, and she's always trying to help make the town better."

The mayor must have seen the confusion on Colton's face

because he smiled and then let out a deep laugh. He wrapped an arm around Colton's shoulders, which was a feat with Colton being over six feet tall. "You have a lot to learn, my young man. There are elected leaders that help a community, but there are also those who have such a way about them that they shape the decisions that impact a small community such as ours."

"You're telling me that some young woman has enough sway to persuade four thousand people?" Had he stepped into the Twilight Zone? He'd seen the town council in his hometown work together to make changes back when he was in high school, but he'd never thought one young woman could have such a profound effect on the rest of the town.

"Just don't make her mad. That's my one piece of advice for you." The man chuckled before walking out the door.

"Basically, I win over the girl and I win the contract?" Colton called out before the mayor disappeared.

The man turned and nodded. "Exactly. Good luck, Mr. Maxfield."

Colton ran his hands over his face, wishing he could be working on one of the projects he was used to back in Denver. But this was a new opportunity for him, the chance to move up in the company and become a project manager instead of just a finish carpenter. With a pay raise came several improved prospects.

Of course, while overseeing this project, Colton would also be expected to put in some of the manual labor. Adam already told him that with all the jobs going on in Denver, he'd be hiring newbies to start on the development out here. That meant Colton would have to keep plugging away as the craftsman he'd become over the past twelve years, training workers on the way Dream Homes did things. He didn't mind it much, but he knew he couldn't do that kind of work for the rest of his life.

And all that could be a pipe dream if this didn't go through. Colton's mind flashed to Becca's irritated face, and he groaned. If he wasn't supposed to make her mad, he was definitely off on the wrong foot.

Walking out of Town Hall, Becca blew out a deep breath. Just what she needed in her life, some big lunkhead coming in and thinking he could disrupt the entire balance of Sage Creek. She'd hoped the mayor would set him straight, but with the man's determination to have this project approved, she could see the mayor giving the construction worker pointers on how to win over the town.

She just needed to focus on getting the orders in for all the flowers she'd need for the wedding this weekend, the Founder's Day Festival, and Mother's day.

"Becca, did you just get out of the meeting?" Susie Jones stood before her, the picture of perfection, if there was such a thing. Her dark brown hair fell to her waist in loose curls, and her outfit looked as though she could step on a runway at any moment. Susie had gone to school with Becca but was a few years younger. She'd stayed in Sage Creek after graduation, taking a job at the bank soon after. At the beginning of the year, she'd taken over the bridal shop in town as Stacy Carston was ready to retire to a year-round tropical climate.

"Yep. The meeting just got out. Are you looking for some-one?" Becca glanced back to the building, trying to remember every person who'd been in regular chairs. None were related to Susie, and all the men were old enough to be her father.

"No. Okay, well, yeah," she said, tucking her hair behind one ear. "There's a guy who walked in and looked pretty amazing. I gave him directions to the room before I left the city building. You had to have seen him. I think he's from out of town."

Becca rolled her eyes. Leave it to Susie to only worry about a guy when their small town was hanging in the balance. She turned to look at the entrance just as that Colton guy walked out of the building. "You mean him?"

Susie nodded emphatically. "Yes, it was definitely him. Isn't he scrumptious?"

He's not a dessert, Susie.

Normally, Becca might agree with her. He was tall and broad-shouldered, and his voice was smooth as chocolate to her ears. Now she was just as bad as the girl next to her. Except she knew his motives, and she wasn't going to be swayed by his good looks, even if he did check quite a few of her boxes. The similarities between him and Peter were too great, and she had to stay focused on saving the town from disruption.

Susie touched Becca's arm, pulling her out of a quick daydream. "I think I'll say hi before I head home." She gave Becca a little wave as she walked over to where the new guy was standing.

Stomping off down the street, Becca fumed. The sting of changing the town she loved so dearly, even by a few dozen homes, didn't sit well with her.

This was her oasis, her town of peace. She didn't need someone to come in and interrupt that, especially not a guy from the big city. She just needed to make sure the council voted no next week. What could she do to convince people? She'd need a plan and a darn good one to make sure the council members sided with her.

David Wallaby might agree with her, but for entirely different reasons. She'd been half-grateful for his comments during the meeting, but then he kept talking. Maybe it was good they hadn't voted today. As she ticked through the members of the council, she realized how many people were already for the subdivision. She'd need to start working on each of them throughout the next week.

Becca's stomach growled, and she knew she'd need sustenance to create any in-depth plans to thwart the subdivision. After debating whether or not to cook at home, she turned and walked down to the Sage Creek Diner just west of her flower shop.

Pulling open the door, she was hit by the familiar smells of meat, potatoes, and pie, all of which sounded amazing right then.

"Becca, how are we doing today?" Velda asked from behind the large counter. A woman in her late fifties or early sixties, she'd been running this place since Becca could remember. She'd been a friend of Becca's mom, and Becca remembered how the two could sit and talk all day if they didn't have anything going on.

Just the thought caused the tears to rush to Becca's eyes, and she blinked them away. She wasn't usually so emotional, but it seemed as if everything reminded her of her parents the past few days.

Sitting on one of the turning stools at the bar, Becca rested her hands on the countertop, bottling up her emotions. As much as she loved the owner, she wasn't in the mood to have any deep discussions, especially when the place was fairly packed.

"Going all right, Velda. Can I get the French dip sandwich?"

"Of course, dear. Anything interesting go on at the council meeting?" Velda pushed a rag around the countertop, wiping the same section over and over again.

Rolling her eyes, Becca nodded and leaned forward, lowering her voice. "A guy from Denver came to get approval for plans to build down on the old Johnson farm."

"I think I saw him when I came to open up for lunch. He's a handsome man, don't you think, Becca?" The glint in her eye caused Becca to shake her head, trying not to smile. As much as she hated being set up on dates by the locals, Velda was much better in that area than most.

Becca groaned. "Don't get me started, Velda. He's trying to change the town. You know I couldn't be with someone who wants to disrupt life here in our perfect little haven."

Velda leaned forward and gave her a sympathetic smile. "Life can go on, dear girl. Peter wasn't right for you. That doesn't mean every guy is going to disappoint you."

As much as Becca didn't want to agree with that statement, she felt the truth of it hit her in the chest. She'd never really forgiven Peter for leaving her at the altar over a year ago. They'd planned to get married near the anniversary of her family's death. Now, instead of a celebration of a new life to help get her through that tough time, she had one more memory to slice through her as she reflected over her life.

Deciding to avoid the direct comment, Becca said, "We vote on it next week. I just hope the town realizes we don't need new development. We have everything we need already."

"In some ways, yes. But there are several things we don't have. It would be nice to have a movie theater to see some of the newer movies when they come out. Or a bigger grocery store," Velda said with a shrug. "There are always advantages on the other side of the disadvantages, Becca. Just remember that."

Another citizen who was Team Development. Becca would have to hone her persuasive speech or she'd be pushing everyone to the other side.

Velda turned away, calling out the order of the French dip sandwich to the chef in back.

Becca pulled out her phone, trying to get her mind to wind down a bit. The tulips still had a few weeks of blooming to go, but she made a note to order more at the end of May. She could grow a lot of flowers in the garden she'd created in her backyard, but sometimes it was better to supplement with shipments from other flower nurseries nearby. Tulips were the first thing most guys asked for when buying flowers for their wives, and she often wondered if it was the only one they knew besides roses.

She felt the air move when someone sat down on the stool next to her. Not wanting to look up at first, she swiped and clicked some more on her phone. There were how many stools empty? They couldn't have chosen one a few seats away?

Velda came out with a cup of hot chocolate for Becca and then turned to the person next to her. "What can I get you, handsome? I'm Velda." The woman's voice had changed, and Becca looked up with a groan. Colton.

"Hi, Velda. I'm Colton. Do you have a turkey club?" he asked in that deep baritone voice.

Becca opened her mouth, ready to ask Velda for a takeout box. She did not want to be sitting by him through all of her dinner.

"We sure do, hun. Anything else?" Velda winked in his direction, and Becca's mouth dropped open. First Susie and now Velda? She hoped the people would look at the facts of the subdivision rather than the man's sheer size. And strong jaw. And dreamy chocolate-brown eyes.

Becca looked away and took a sip of her hot chocolate, hoping the sweetness would distract her from the thoughts racing through her head. She was supposed to be annoyed with him, not admiring his features.

"Rough meeting today, huh?" It took a minute for Becca to realize he was talking to her, and while she wanted to turn up her nose and move to another spot in the diner, she knew her mother would roll over in her grave if she heard her daughter belittle some newcomer.

"That's actually quite tame for our council meetings. One time, Jerry Porter brought his horse into Town Hall. When it got spooked, several things were broken, and Jerry ended up with a broken collar bone."

The smile on his face made her thaw somewhat, but she knew she'd have to be firm and not let some city boy soften her up. She couldn't let him get to her. The town depended on her for that at least.

"So, what is there to do for fun here?" Colton asked, his dark brown eyes fixed on hers. She was grateful Velda brought her French dip right then so she could break her gaze away. "It seems I'll be in town longer than I expected."

Taking a bite, Becca chewed and swallowed before patting her lips with a napkin. A quick internal debate about whether she should even risk talking to him was won over by the idea that Sage Creek was about hospitality, no matter what the person was there for.

"There's quite a bit of everything. We have local game nights where a bunch of people join up to play board games. You can go swimming in Sage Creek pond just up through the pine trees behind Town Hall. And there are some good hiking trails up there."

"And?"

She should have bitten her tongue at that point, but her patience was wearing thin, and she let the words fly. "We're not a big city with dozens of things to entertain you, Mr. Maxfield, and if that's what you're thinking, you may as well go right back to Denver. If you're more adventurous, you'll find that we create a lot of our own fun by sheer imagination."

Turning to take another bite of her sandwich, she tried to hide the smile caused by the slack-jawed expression on his face. A surge of satisfaction flowed through her. She just wished the guy sitting next to her was Peter and that she'd finally given him a piece of her mind.

"You're right," Colton said after a minute or two. "I may have been a little small-minded. Would you mind showing me around tomorrow? I could use a tour guide."

Becca stopped chewing mid-bite and slowly turned to look at him. Swallowing, she asked, "You want *me* to take you around town?"

"Yeah, if you wouldn't mind. It seems like you know the people and most of what goes on in this town."

Dropping her voice to a whisper, Becca said, "Are you trying to say I'm the town gossip?"

Colton sat back with his hands in the air, his eyes as wide as when he mentioned he'd forgotten the test documents during the meeting. "That's not what I meant; I promise. What I meant was that you seem to know a lot of people, and you might be able to give me the best history of Sage Creek. Help me understand this place."

This guy was a smooth talker. She'd have to keep her guard up if she was to make an impact on derailing the subdivision. But maybe spending time with him would show her some of the weaknesses that would come with the development.

"It would have to be after work. I own the flower shop on the next block over on the corner of Fourth and Main."

Colton's eyes narrowed as he studied her face. "Flower girl, huh? What made you decide to go into flowers?"

"If you want a tour of the place, stop asking so many questions," Becca said, pursing her lips. "Meet me at the flower shop at three tomorrow." She called over the counter, "Velda, put this on my tab. I'll be by tomorrow with the money."

With that, she stood and walked out of the diner, her stomach protesting that she should've gotten a to-go box.

Why were men so infuriating? Especially the ones who didn't enjoy the small-town life?

CHAPTER 4

Colton stared at Becca's nearly untouched plate as he thought through their conversation, feeling bad that he'd run her off before she could eat. Was the subdivision the only reason she disliked him so much?

He was grateful when Velda brought his sandwich to the counter. She seemed to eye him for a minute before turning to get something from the back. Taking a bite of the sandwich, he savored the flavors. He hadn't had one this good in quite some time, the thick bacon and perfectly sliced tomato mixing well with the mayonnaise, turkey, and lettuce. At least the food in the small town was good, even if the residents were a little crazy.

As if deciding to finally talk to him, Velda stepped up to the counter. Colton grabbed a napkin from the holder in front of him and wiped his mouth as he looked up at her.

"Becca's not always like that."

With a frown, he said, "Like what?"

"Ornery. Snappy." Velda had one eyebrow raised, as if waiting for him to catch up.

"Okay." He wasn't sure why she was telling him this.

Dipping his head, he took another bite of the sandwich, trying to chew quietly. He felt Velda's eyes boring into his head and looked back up, nodding at her. He didn't want to be rude, but he also didn't want to keep thinking about the woman who smelled of fragrant flowers and had a gaze that pulled him in.

Velda smiled. "She's just a little worried about things changing around here. She lost her family a few years ago, and she thinks if things don't change, it will be like they're still here with her. Sometimes, I think she's holding on too hard and won't be able to move on."

Colton looked around, still unsure why he, a stranger to Sage Creek, needed to know any of that. He was just here to do a job, not get involved in the local dynamic.

But then the mayor's words rang through his mind, and he nodded. It seemed if he was going to crack the hard layer that was Becca Taylor, he was going to have to change tactics.

"I own this place, by the way," Velda said, circling her finger as if to encompass the entire building. "Anytime you need anything, just come on in. I'm here to help." She smiled at him and walked to the other side of the bar to fill a water cup for another customer.

Colton finished his sandwich and fries, going over the events from the day. Seeing the plate of unfinished food next to him, he waved Velda over. "Will you box this up? It seems I need to make a peace offering." He paid for both his meal and Becca's, along with a tip.

"Can you tell me where I might find Becca?" he asked the older woman.

With a mischievous grin, Velda said, "Of course, darlin'. Just head straight down Fourth and cross Main Street. Hers is the first house on the right."

As he walked out the door of the diner, he heard her say, "Good luck."

He took a few steps, taking in the beauty of the night sky. The moon was full, and the stars seemed close enough to touch. He'd never seen anything like it. In Denver, he didn't take much time to look, but he knew they were never this bright.

Following Velda's instructions, Colton stopped in front of the white two-story house. It was well-kept from what he could see in the moonlight, and it fit her. He smiled as he realized she lived right next to the flower shop. Not a long commute there.

Raising his hand, he knocked on the door and then took a step back. He looked down at his shirt and swiped at a glob of mayo that must have fallen out of his sandwich. The door opened, the light behind backlighting the person at the door.

"What are you doing here?" Becca asked. She flipped a switch for the porch lights and pulled her arms across her chest.

"I figured you were probably still hungry, and I felt bad if I was the cause of you leaving so abruptly." He held out the Styrofoam container to her, and she hesitated, looking between him and the container for several seconds before reaching out and taking it.

Her hazel eyes glanced up at him again, and when Colton tried to breathe in, something in his chest hitched. With her hair pulled up into a ponytail on the top of her head and dressed in sweats and a t-shirt, she looked beautiful even while comfortable.

"Uh, thank you. You really didn't have to do that." Her words were soft, as if surprised by something so simple.

Colton shrugged. "It wasn't a big deal." He paused a moment, trying to decide where to go from there. Part of him wished she would invite him in, giving him an opportunity to get to know her better. But he realized they were to tour the town the next day. That would be enough. He didn't need to start tangling his emotions already. The subdivision wasn't a done deal, and even if it passed, it was best to keep his heart from going through the wringer when he'd have to eventually leave Sage Creek.

"I'm going to head back to the hotel, but I'll be at your shop tomorrow at three." He smiled at her, hoping she'd at least acknowledge the appointment they'd set for the next day.

"Sounds good. I'll have to brush up on my town history while I finish my food." Colton watched as the corners of her mouth teased a smile before revealing her bright white teeth. Her face lit up with the smile, and it took him a few moments to realize he was staring at her awkwardly.

Nodding his head, Colton waved and stepped down one step on the porch. "Good luck with that. I expect to be winning any trivia tournaments you have here by the end of the tour."

She chuckled, the light laughter making him join in. A few seconds later, she shut the door, and Colton felt like he'd been released from some trance.

As he walked down the road back to his hotel, he thought about the mayor's and Velda's words about Becca. He'd caught a few different sides to her already, but maybe there was some hope that he could at least sway her vote to his side.

CHAPTER 5

$\mathcal{B}$ecca sat on the couch, unable to concentrate on the show she'd been watching when she heard the knock at the door. The unopened yogurt container she'd pulled from the fridge once she arrived home sat on the side table, and she opened the box Colton had just dropped off.

She'd judged him several times since that morning, always for the negative, but what man thought about a girl he'd just met? Placing a fry into her mouth, Becca smiled at the memory of her interactions with Colton throughout the day. They'd gone from bumping into one another outside the flower shop on her way to the coffee shop, to the council meeting where she'd been less than kind, and finally to the diner and her front step.

It had been a while since she'd gone through such a range of emotions, but the guy who stood on her porch intrigued her. Sure, she probably shouldn't think about him as incredibly attractive and surprisingly kind as it would derail her plans, but in all her years, she'd never had a man think about something so simple yet so impressive.

Peter had been all wrong for her, something she'd come

to understand in the last few months, but there had been so many good qualities about him at first. They'd just gotten swallowed up by his need to join the rat race of the big cities.

Her thoughts were cut off by the ringtone signaling her best friend, Danielle Holloway, a news station reporter and journalist working on a story in Europe.

Becca swallowed the bite of her sandwich before answering the call. "Dani! What are you doing up this early? It's ten at night here, so it's like…" Becca paused, trying to do the time calculation in her head.

"Five in the morning. We're heading out on an early morning hike before we start filming for the station. I figured I'd try and catch you before my tour moves out for the day. How are things there?"

"Not as amazing as traveling to Europe for 'research' for your next book. At least, you better be getting more ideas for that novel you've always wanted to write. Why not when you didn't have to pay to go there." She ended the sentence with sarcasm, and Dani laughed.

"Hey, I'm not complaining. It's amazing over here. I wish you would've come, just to get out of town for a little while." The tone in Dani's voice caused the irritation from earlier to flare up again.

Clearing her throat, Becca said, "I'm good here. I don't need to die in an airplane accident."

A moment of silence echoed over the line, and Dani's voice came a bit softer. "You won't die if you leave town. I promise. But I'm not spending an arm and a leg to debate over you leaving Sage Creek. Why are you so annoyed?"

"I'm not annoyed." The words came out with a bite, and Becca winced, feeling bad for lashing out at her friend halfway across the world.

"Uh-huh. Spill."

What friend would take the time to call internationally

while enjoying a work trip around Europe? Danielle. They'd been best friends since middle school, and she'd been Becca's lifeline since the accident, always there when Becca needed to vent about the loss of her family or how her life wasn't turning out how she'd like it to. But as much as she encouraged Becca to venture out of the small town, Becca had yet to leave the boundaries of Dalton County since her family died. She'd come home for the funeral and simply stayed.

Becca gave her the condensed version of meeting Colton and his plans for ruining the town. She tried to water down him appearing with her food, hoping Danielle wouldn't see too much into it. But she should have figured Danielle's investigative abilities would shine through. It was the journalist in her after all.

"What does this Colton look like?" Becca could picture the playful look on her friend's face, curiosity directing the questions.

"Dark brown hair, dark brown eyes, over six feet tall."

"Thick build?"

Becca told her yes, and Dani laughed. "So, he's basically Peter, only a slightly different version."

Squeezing her eyes shut, Becca nodded, even though Dani couldn't see her.

"Are you afraid he'll be just like Peter?"

"Why would I be afraid of that? It's not like he's moving to Sage Creek."

Dani scoffed. "Becca, at some point, you're going to have to get over that man. He was an idiot to leave you like he did, but you can't hold that against every strapping guy who is a builder by profession. And the fact that Colton brought you the food you didn't eat...I'm giving him serious brownie points for that."

"Strapping guy? Who says that?" Becca said with a laugh.

Then she paused, and in a more serious tone, she said, "I'm not ready for a relationship, Dani."

"I'm not saying you are either, but there's a difference to being nice and being rude. You're acting like we're in the fifth grade and you can't be nice to Lloyd Jefferson because he'll want to marry you. Just be nice. I know it's in there somewhere."

Becca snorted. "I think it's been buried."

"I'll be home next week. Mrs. Watkins will tell me if you've been nice or not. Don't think I won't ask her."

"Thanks, Mom," Becca said sarcastically, going somber directly after.

"You're going to be fine, Becca. One day at a time. Use that charming smile I know is in there somewhere. Who knows? Maybe getting to know him will help you find a way to stop the subdivision, if that's what you really want to do."

"Of course I want it to stop." Becca chewed on the side of her lip as her thoughts raced over Danielle's words. "You might have a point there, though. Thanks for being awesome."

Danielle chuckled. "What's a best friend for? Okay, I've got to run and meet up with the group for the hike. Good luck, and I'll see you soon."

After hanging up, Becca slowly finished her sandwich, her thoughts bouncing between Danielle's words and the attractive builder. Maybe time with him wouldn't be a lost cause. The town was depending on her sound judgment to get past this. And by telling herself she was just looking for ammunition against the plans, she could be sure her heart was locked up tight.

CHAPTER 6

The night was long and quiet, making it difficult for Colton to sleep again. By the time three in the afternoon rolled around, Colton was dragging, the lack of sleep over the past two nights weighing on him. He walked through town and stood in front of a shop called The Flower Girl. He smiled, the simplicity of the name seeming to fit the little he knew about Becca.

He entered the store and saw several people still in line behind the register as Becca flitted from the front to the back to the front again. She brought a bouquet of pink flowers to a woman at the front of the line, ringing her out before moving on to the next order.

Colton froze, not sure what he should do. Should he leave and come back? Or offer to do something he knew nothing about?

Deciding on the latter and striding up to her, he saw her jaw tense as she glanced in his direction. "Is there something I can do to help?" he asked.

Her eyes widened, searching his face to see if he was serious. "Do you know anything about flowers?"

Giving her a wry grin, Colton said, "Does buying them for other people count?"

Becca rolled her eyes and shook her head. She waved for him to follow her into the back room. "No, that does not count. You've probably gotten the advice of the florist on those occasions."

Colton snapped his fingers and pointed at her, emphasizing that she was correct. He'd only ever bought flowers for his mother, but it seemed like the advice he'd been given had worked out because she always loved the arrangements he'd given her. Turning serious, he looked at the long workbench covered in bits of flowers and several tools. "What can I do?"

"Cut the ends of these flowers about an inch, but do it at a diagonal. Let me go see what Carl Sturgis wants, and I'll be right back."

Grateful she left an example, Colton picked up the scissors and tried to imitate the look at the bottoms of the long-stemmed red roses. He'd almost finished the dozen by the time she came back in.

"That actually looks pretty good," she said, sounding surprised.

"You do know that I'm a finish carpenter, right? Pretty good doesn't cut it in my line of work."

Her eyebrows came together as she frowned like she didn't really understand what he was talking about. She walked to pull out some other flowers from the cooler. Placing those on the work table, she nudged Colton out of the way to reach the roses. Her hand grazed his forearm, sending little volts of electricity through him. He'd never felt that before. Maybe he'd just created too much static from shuffling back and forth next to the long table.

Colton hadn't noticed the wall of ribbon and paper to his right, everything neatly lined up. Becca pulled at the end of a thick piece of white ribbon and wrapped it around the roses, her fingers flying as they tied a bow. She fiddled with it for a moment, straightening it in spots. Pulling a long box out from a stack under the wall of ribbon, she folded the box before placing the flowers inside.

This time, she pulled on a deep red ribbon with a decorative edging and wrapped it around the box. Picking up the box, she disappeared up front again.

Maybe he wasn't used to women who were good with crafts and design, but he was stunned by the speed with which she'd been able to wrap it.

He looked down at the colored flowers, wondering what needed to be done to them. She reappeared just as he picked up one of the yellow flowers, looking at him as though he'd just been caught for something. She pulled out a vase from a shelf next to the work table and gathered several of the flowers already out, sticking them one at a time into the container.

"I have this arrangement and then one more order, and I'll be done for the day."

"Sounds good." Colton leaned against a cabinet and folded his arms, watching her work. It was as if she had a certain instinct for where the flowers would look best, and after several minutes, the colorful bouquet was ready to go out.

"How did you learn how to do all this?" Colton asked, unable to keep his question to himself. It was like putting a puzzle together without a picture as a guide, and he admired the talent it took for her to do that.

Becca pulled out a small box with several pieces of fake green leaves. "My mother always loved flowers. I used to watch her coming up with different creations and try to mimic her movements. I don't have half the talent she had, but I love seeing people's reactions to flowers and how happy it can make them."

After trimming three flowers up to the bud, she wrapped them quickly with wire, adding in a sprig of that small white flower everyone used. The finished creation was a corsage.

"Is there a dance going on or something?" he asked, pointing to the corsage.

Becca turned to him, shining her bright smile, but he could see her gaze was on a memory more than anything in the room. "No, Mr. Greeley just likes to give his wife a wrist corsage every year for their anniversary. I've been making them since my shop opened."

"What did he do before that?"

Becca paused and turned to him. "I've never really thought about it. We didn't have an official flower shop in town before I opened this one. Most folks would ask my mom for something or go to the next town over."

"Does this town sustain the flower shop by itself?"

She placed one finger up, carrying the vase and the box to the front of the store. A few minutes ticked by, and she reappeared through the swinging door.

With a hand on her hip, she leaned against the large table, and her eyes locked onto his. "What was your question?"

"Do you have enough business in this small town?"

Colton watched as she put her tongue to the roof of her mouth, her eyes drifting to the ceiling. "Most of the time, yes. My best friend gave me the idea to do a subscription-type service, and most of the offices in town have taken me up on it. They get a new arrangement of flowers every week or two for a flat fee. That keeps life afloat when money is tight and people don't want to splurge on flowers."

She began tidying up, almost running to pick up papers and extra leaves and petals from the floor. Colton helped, grabbing some of the short stems that had fallen off the table from when he'd helped.

He didn't see or hear her near his vicinity when they both

reached for the same leaf at the same time. That same electric charge tingled through his hand, and he looked up, seeing the surprise on her face. Did she feel the same thing? What was it about this town that was making him so jumpy? He was usually the definition of calm and collected. But something about this place, this girl, had him questioning everything he'd known before.

She led him to the front room and untied her apron and hung it on a hook by the cash register before disappearing out back again. Colton heard a door slam shut and wondered if she'd gone outside altogether.

She appeared a few moments later, standing at the front door of the shop.

"Are you ready to go?" She looked at him expectantly, pulling her long hair into a ponytail. Her blouse looked different, but Colton wasn't sure he could remember what she'd been wearing before that.

"How'd you do that?"

A wide grin spread across her face. "Magic." She waited a few seconds before saying, "I had to run over to the house and grab my wallet."

"I saw that you live next door when I brought your food last night. I guess you don't have to worry about being late to the office." He chuckled, and she shook her head with a half-smile.

She opened the door and waited until he walked out before closing it and locking up.

Colton gave her a small smile. "I'm surprised you lock up in such a small town."

A blush reached her cheeks, and Becca looked up at him. "A habit I picked up from college. I learned the hard way that not everyone in the world is the most honest."

"Robbed?"

She nodded. "I forgot to lock up as I went to class, and

someone came in and took our TV and a bunch of other expensive stuff my roommates had. I was just glad I'd taken my laptop to class. I couldn't afford another one, and it had my term paper saved on it." She turned and looked up and down Main Street.

Colton was surprised she'd opened up to him a bit more, not the wall she'd been the day before. Maybe he was making progress with her. "Where did you go to school?"

Something passed over her face, and all of the excitement and happiness he'd seen from her over the past thirty minutes vanished.

"So, you want to see the town, right?" she asked, ignoring his question.

When he nodded, she turned to the right. "That's the doctor's office," she said, pointing to the building to the north of the flower shop, located on Fourth Street. "The library is next to that, with one of the town parks behind it."

She turned to face the other side of Main Street. "The hardware store is there across the street from my shop, and behind it, on Fourth Street, is the Sage Creek Diner where we ate dinner last night." She stopped talking and looked a bit flustered. "Thanks for bringing my food over, by the way. Yesterday was…an off day for me, and I really appreciate it." Her eyes looked more green right then, and the small, awkward smile she gave him caused him to smile wider.

"Again, no worries. Us city folk, as you call us, do have some manners." He winked at her, and she shook her head, trying to keep from smiling.

"Anyway, if you plan to build here, you might want to talk to Tanner Hart. He's the owner of the hardware store. It would go a long way with the townspeople if they had a part in helping with the buildings, whether through materials or use of their businesses." Her eyes widened, and she clamped her mouth shut as if she'd said too much.

"I'll keep that in mind. For someone who's against the growth, you sure do make sure the town is taken care of." Colton smiled at the hurried steps Becca took across Fourth Street as though trying to catch up with something.

She pointed catty-corner from her store. "We have a plumber and air-conditioning guy across the street there—Tuck Sanders. Next to him on Fourth Street is the bridal shop."

Colton touched her arm and felt nothing but zaps of electricity pulse through his fingers. "This town supports a bridal shop?" He'd only meant to touch her in disbelief that a specialty store like that could survive with so few town members. "Do you really have that many weddings around here?"

Her eyes flashed, and her lips pursed as she raised her chin just a little. "You'd be surprised what we can sustain here."

Weddings and college seemed to be buttons for this woman. He'd have to remember that if he wanted his plan of gaining her trust to succeed.

She turned and continued down Main Street, pointing to the next block on the opposite side of the road. "The elementary and middle school are on this block. The one you see on the corner is the elementary, and the middle school is on the back side. Most of the kids go to high school over in Greeley. They have to be bussed there. West of the schools, we have an indoor sports facility for our Rec Department that we also use as a cultural hall. Our hospital, on Second Street, and fairgrounds, down from the flower shop on Fourth Street, are on the east side of town."

"Do you have a lot of events out here?"

"You'd be surprised. We have the Founder's Day Festival coming up in a few weeks, and then the county fair is just before school gets started. To be honest, the town celebrates just about everything. The ladies like any excuse to try out their baking skills."

That was something he could get behind. He hadn't gotten a lot of good homemade meals or desserts since his mother had been ill. His meager attempt at cooking, while healthier on a consistent basis, did nothing to rival the memories of the feasts his mother could cook when she was able to work.

"Did you like growing up here?" he asked, suddenly curious. He watched her face, wondering if this was going to be another taboo subject.

She nodded, her eyes on the ground in front of them as they continued walking. "I did. It was eye-opening to leave for school, but it just made me that much more grateful for the childhood I had." She choked up a little bit and paused a moment before continuing on, putting on the mask he'd seen a few times in the last twenty-four hours.

"Main Street dead-ends at Town Hall, but you've already been there," she said as they walked up the street. "To the east of it are the police and fire stations. Another restaurant, the post office and newspaper, our gas station, and the grocery stores are back on the south end of town near the hotel you're—"

"You have more than one grocery store in a town this small?" he asked, cutting her off.

She frowned at him. "You act so surprised with all of this. I doubt anyone would have started these businesses and kept them running for several years without doing some research." She shook her head, letting out a long breath. When she spoke again, her tone had settled somewhat, and Colton couldn't hide his grin. "There are a lot of smaller farms nearby, and this way, they don't have to go all the way to the big city to do their shopping."

She stopped at the side of the fountain in front of Town

Hall, the gurgling of the water catching his attention. "This was put in about ten years ago. There was a bus accident, and several high school students were killed." Emotion filled her voice on the last few words, and she opened her mouth to say more but shut it, staring into the fountain.

"Were you related to one of the students?" Colton asked, trying to keep his tone soft.

Becca's head swiveled in his direction. She ran a finger under her nose as she sniffed. "No, sorry. Just memories of this place. Let's keep going."

Waiting for him to follow, she walked along the road that wound around behind Town Hall, passing the parking lot he'd parked in the night before. When she walked through the gates of a wrought iron fence, he was confused. Shouldn't they be heading in the opposite direction back down Main Street to complete the tour?

"Where are we going?" he finally asked.

"You'll see. It's my favorite part of this town." She followed a path that led through some pine trees, and for a second, Colton looked back at the town, hoping this wasn't some plot to get rid of the guy trying to expand their population. He had to laugh at the thought. There's no way she could pin him down.

As he walked along, he admired the beauty around them. Several birds flew past, and the pine trees made for a beautiful landscape. He was in fairly good shape from all the manual labor of his job, but the sudden steepness of the incline caused him to take an extra breath here and there. Becca was way up ahead of him now, and once he made it to the crest of one of the hills, he saw her standing, head back, facing the sun.

By the time he'd caught up with her, he breathed in deeply, trying to regain some of the air he'd lost on the way up. He glanced at the scenery, taking a step back to admire it like a painting. A large pond, more like a lake, sat in the middle of the grove of trees with mountains as a backdrop. He'd never seen anything like it before.

"This is amazing."

"Yes, it is. This is Sage Creek Pond. It's one of the favorites of the local families, and not many outsiders know about it." She turned and waved a hand at the trees. "The pines block the view of the town, but it also keeps this as a safe haven."

"I'm surprised you showed me if it's your favorite spot. Since I'm an out-of-towner." He said it with sarcasm, waiting for her reaction.

When she finally turned to him, she looked deep into his eyes, a solemnness to her features. Colton worked to not flinch away from her gaze. "I'm hoping that when you see something like this, you'll realize how important it is to keep our small town small. With large populations come problems and destruction of beauty."

"I can see why you think that way, but without allowing growth, your small town won't survive the next twenty years."

Becca pinched her eyebrows together and scrunched her nose. "With a rise in population comes the rise of alcohol abuse and vandalism." She stepped closer, her height seeming to grow a couple of inches with the passion in her words.

"But more people can contribute to the overall economy, increasing the standard of living for everyone in the community." He smiled as she thought about that for a moment. A mixture of pine and lavender filled his nose, and he couldn't keep his gaze away from her lips. The pinkness of them caused him to lick his own.

She pointed to something across the lake. "Maybe that's true, but I still don't like it." A blush crept to her cheeks, and the thought crossed his mind to erase the distance between them and see how her lips felt on his. But she took a step back, breaking the current that ran between them.

Becca motioned to the mountains. "You can take a walk on the path around the lake, or if you like to hike, there are several trails that start just over there. Just make sure someone knows where you went so we can come find you if need be."

Colton couldn't help but grin. "Would you be worried about me?"

From the look on her face, she knew he was being obnoxious, but something in him just wouldn't stop. She had to be the world's best avoider of questions, as there were at least five she hadn't answered in their time together that day.

A sly grin appeared, and she said, "It's too early to tell."

Shaking her head, she moved back the direction they'd come, walking down the dirt path. He fell into step with her, studying her features from the corner of his eye.

"You're lucky that my mother's voice is still in my head after all this time," she said, one corner of her mouth turning up. "I only agreed to give you a tour of the town because that's what she would have wanted me to do."

"Well, it sounds like she was a great woman." Colton stuffed his hands into his pants pockets, trying to come up with something more to talk about. He liked the variety of expressions she used as she spoke, and he'd hoped to avoid more silence from her.

Becca stopped at the bottom of the path, turning to him with her eyes boring into his. "What do you get out of the subdivision?"

Colton leaned back on his heels, surprised by the bluntness of the question. "What do you mean? It's my job to secure this build job."

"So you won't be getting any special awards if it goes

through?" Becca's arms crossed over her chest, the action giving off the intimidating factor she was probably going for.

With a quick shrug, Colton moved his boot back and forth over the dirt. "I go from being the grunt man to directing the work on projects. It's a step up, but it's not like the company is giving me millions of dollars for it." Glancing up, he asked, "Why does that matter?"

"It just seems like you're trying really hard to get me to like you. I'd like to be optimistic and hope that it's because you're a nice guy and you actually care about learning about the town. But there's a part of me that thinks it's to sway my vote. I'm not the kind to fall easily, Colton Maxfield, so if that's your intention, don't waste your time."

Colton opened his mouth to say something, finding nothing coherent connecting from his brain to his mouth. Was he really that predictable? "Whoa! I wasn't expecting that when I asked for a tour. Obviously, being new to Sage Creek, I don't know that many people, especially ones that are close to our age. I just thought it would be fun to pass the time learning about the town."

Becca's eyes narrowed, searching his face for several seconds. She didn't seem to find anything because her features softened. "Sorry, there have been people who take advantage of this town, and I just don't want to see it all ruined." She turned and walked down the rest of the path.

He caught up to her and, wanting to keep their conversation going a bit longer, said, "Who took advantage of you? Was it in college?"

For a moment, she looked vulnerable, like a memory had resurfaced, and her eyes filled with tears.

Colton took a few tentative steps toward Becca and wrapped his arms around her, pulling her in. She didn't resist, leaning her head against his chest. For several seconds, he just breathed, feeling like his nerves were on fire and everything was right in the world.

Then, without warning, her whole body stiffened, and she paused. Without a word, she pulled away and ran off around the town building and out of sight.

"Way to go, Colton. There goes your chance of being a project manager."

Not ready to head back to his hotel room, Colton sat on the bench next to the water fountain, looking down Main Street. He kept replaying all that had happened during the tour, how drawn he was to Becca, especially up near the pond when they'd embraced. He'd never had a girlfriend long enough to fall in love, and as he thought about it, the last one he had was just a couple years after high school. But had it been so long ago that the crackling chemistry between he and Becca was so foreign?

He could still feel her in his arms, like a puzzle piece he hadn't realized he'd been missing. She tried to be so strong, but under the mask she put on, there had to be a lot of hurt. He just hoped he could avoid hurting her. Even though his mother rarely talked about his father, he knew how much it hurt her that he'd just up and left all those years ago.

In the middle of that thought, his phone rang, and he pulled it out of his pocket. Adam preferred to call by video chat, and Colton wasn't sure he was in the mood for that right now. But if he didn't pick up, his boss would keep calling until he did.

Swiping on the screen, he said, "Hey, Adam. How's it going?"

"Great, man. What's the scoop over there in the country?" Adam looked like he was in his office and kept checking himself out on the screen, combing his hair in the right direction.

"Not much. I went to the town council meeting last night and delivered the plans. They're going to take this week to look them over and come to a decision next Tuesday."

Adam bobbed his head up and down. "Okay, that's not a bad thing. What's the overall feeling you get from the people?"

Colton hesitated a moment, trying to decide how to say it. "I don't have a really good count since they didn't actually vote. I know the mayor is all for us building, but there are for sure two holdouts."

"Do what you've got to do, then," Adam said, pointing his finger at the camera as if trying to poke Colton. "We need this project to go through so we don't look like commercial giants anymore. I really want our residential department to take off."

With a frown, Colton said, "What are you talking about? Our residential building has been doing well for years. It's only increased since I started working for you."

"But we've got to amp it up, and the perfect way to do that is by starting with a charming small town. What are you doing until the vote?"

Colton swallowed, feeling guilty. "I've just been trying to get to know some of the people in town, hoping it will help when it comes time to vote. But I can come back and work on something if you need."

"No, man. That sounds like a good use of your time. Just lock it up for us, Colt." With that, Adam hung up.

Looking around, Colton suddenly felt self-conscious.

There weren't many people out and about right now, but he hoped no one had overheard anything. Not that there was anything shocking in their conversation, but he didn't like it when Adam talked so cavalierly about things.

Adam had taken over for his father the year before, and while Colton still enjoyed working for Dream Homes, he missed the simplicity of working with Adam's dad. Marcus Summers had built Summers Construction off of several commercial buildings over the years. When Colton joined on, he'd started as the gopher just out of high school and then helped Marcus create Dream Homes three years ago. The smaller entity was thriving more and more every year, but with Adam's appointment as head of the division six months ago, promising rash changes and nearly doubling the amount of buildings being thrown up, Colton just hoped the company could sustain the growth.

Standing, Colton walked past the fountain and down Main Street, stopping on Fourth Street as he glanced at the flower shop and the house next door. Should he go apologize for whatever he'd done to upset Becca? Or was it better that she be alone for the night?

He'd never had to worry about a girl's feelings, as his last girlfriend had never cried in front of him. Being the only child, the one person he'd always worried about was his mother. But something about Becca made him want to comfort her, help her through whatever it was she was going through.

Running a hand through his hair, he shook his head, ready to walk back to the hotel. This was crazy. He'd known the girl two of the three days he'd been in town, and he suddenly felt like he needed to protect her? He searched through the emotions surging through him while he thought of her, trying to find some tie to the subdivision. Nothing.

He'd just have to do his best to keep things professional.

That meant reaching out and giving her a hug, or touching her at all, was off limits from then on.

"Colton!"

He turned at the voice and smiled when he saw the mayor coming toward him.

"How are things this afternoon?" the man asked, putting a hand on Colton's shoulder.

"Going all right, sir. What are you up to?"

Mayor Watkins raised his eyebrows and then the side of his mouth. "Well, I was wondering if you had plans for dinner. Dorothy made more than normal, and she wanted me to invite you over."

Shaking his head, Colton said, "I don't have anything planned. Honestly, a home-cooked meal sounds amazing right now."

"Well, I'm headed that way now. Let's get going. I can smell the garlic bread from here."

*B*ecca ran all the way back to her small house and slammed the door behind her. She skipped several stairs on her way to her bedroom, where she threw herself across the queen bed that barely fit in her old room. She'd run so hard and fast that she hadn't been able to think about the pain spreading through her as memories of college graduation and then her failed wedding took over.

She'd been standing in a large group with her fellow graduates, ready to walk down to the stadium and receive her diploma. She was graduating magna cum laude and hadn't told her parents about it, wanting to see their faces when it was announced.

Someone had called out over the crowd, "Rebecca Taylor!" and she'd waved to signal it was her. She'd had to push through the other graduates to get to one of the professors on the side of the crowd.

He handed her his phone, and she'd put it to her ear, listening as the highway patrolman told her about being called to the scene of an accident and finding her parents and brother at the bottom of a ravine.

Every time she thought about that memory, she felt the same numbness take over, like her world was crumbling to dust and she could only stand on the sidelines and watch it destruct. Dani kept telling her she needed to talk to someone, to find a way to get past it, but that would feel like a betrayal of their memory.

It had been over five years. Why hadn't she been able to cope with the pain? It was the same loop of emotions every time, the excitement of getting out of Sage Creek and exploring the world, and then the accident bringing about a deep sadness, one she couldn't get out of no matter how much she tried to. If she'd only stuck around here and helped her mom open the shop, maybe her family wouldn't have been on the road that day.

Her sadness turned to anger as she thought of Colton, riding in with all his questions. Why did he care? He'd end up with a signed document allowing his company to build, even though she'd valiantly fight for the subdivision to be denied, and then he would leave, just like all the other people she'd loved.

Not that she loved Colton by any means. Not even close. But she'd felt sparks between them, and the way he'd tenderly held her near the pond had sent her heart racing. The smell of the pine trees mixed with an almond scent was stuck in her nose now, long after she'd run off and left him there.

As she thought more about his queries, she could picture the softness in his features. She wanted to tell herself he was just here for the job, that he was only here to sweet-talk her into agreeing to the subdivision plans, but she'd be lying to herself. There was something about him, something earnest and kind, those qualities only enhancing the attraction she felt toward him.

She pushed those thoughts away. Alone and heartbroken

were things she could survive once—okay, twice since Peter's betrayal. But falling for Colton only to have him leave would crush her.

A ball of fur hopped onto the couch and settled in next to Becca, meowing as she ran her fingers along its back. She'd gotten the animal the day after her supposed wedding, naming her for her black and white spots.

"I'm going to keep my distance, Oreo. I'll make sure the city council has all the information they need and keep my feelings professional."

The cat yawned, and Becca chuckled.

You're lonely. Not everything has to end with a happily ever after.

The words were from Danielle, from a conversation shortly after her parents had died. One of the men in town had been asking Becca out at least once a week, and every time Becca had turned him down, he seemed to grow even more courage. She'd finally given the guy one date, which opened the door for when Peter came to town. He'd been contracted to build several homes in the next town over, and at the time, Becca hadn't locked herself down into a no-change type of attitude.

Sure, she was lonely sometimes, and that's when she'd reflect on the past. Peter would usually make an appearance in those memories, and she'd always feel like an idiot as she now saw the signs of his leaving in hindsight. She'd lived in the moment until his departure had caused her to live in the past.

She walked back downstairs and turned on the TV before pulling out a frozen dinner and popping it into the microwave. No, it wasn't the best or healthiest meal, but she wasn't in the mood to cook, and she did not want to run into Colton tonight.

The timer on the microwave beeped, and she pushed the

button to open it. Pulling it out, she wrinkled her nose. The noodles were a little overdone. Grabbing a fork, she made her way to the couch, trying to get into the latest reality TV show.

As her emotions surfaced, she heard her phone ring. Picking it up, she pasted a smile on her face, knowing Dottie would be able to hear the tears if she let them continue.

"Hey, Dottie, how are you?"

"I'm all right, dear. I made too much food again and was hoping you hadn't eaten yet."

Glancing at the shriveled pasta in the cardboard box, Becca said, "I haven't. Let me change, and I'll be over in a few."

Once she got off the phone, she looked down at her shirt, seeing a spot from her drink earlier. No use sitting through a lecture from Dorothy about being neat and tidy. She was ready for something relaxed and fun, and for an older couple, the Watkins could be just that.

CHAPTER 9

The walk wasn't too long as the mayor lived right across the street from Becca. They arrived in front of a white house with a manicured garden and neatly trimmed lawn. "Your house is amazing, Mayor, especially the yard. Do you spend a lot of time working on it?" Colton asked.

The mayor chuckled, his stomach shaking. "Not as much as we probably want to. My wife won't give up working in the garden, but I haven't had time for the lawn in years, so we hire one of the young men down the street. He knows just how we like it. The only problem is, he graduates this year, so we'll see where he ends up. I might have to train a new protégé."

Colton smiled at the thought of some young kid going through training with the mayor. He could only imagine there were a lot of outward appearances to be keeping up with his position in the community.

Turning, Colton looked at the flower shop across the street, with the white two-story house next to it. "You live across from Becca, huh?" he asked, pointing at her house.

The mayor nodded. "Yes, ever since her parents moved in. They first lived on the next street over before coming here. Her mother had such big ideas, and Becca's father made sure to make every one of them happen." He cleared his throat. "We best get into the house. Dottie won't be too happy if the food is cold by the time we arrive."

They walked inside, and Mayor Watkins called out to his wife. The man set his briefcase on the floor next to the door and moved into the kitchen, motioning for Colton to follow. A petite woman stood in front of the stove, stirring something that looked like red sauce.

"I brought us a dinner guest, Dottie." The mayor winked at his wife, and she gave him a sly grin as he bent over to kiss her on the cheek. "Colton, this is my wife, Dottie."

Dottie turned and smiled, wiping her hands on the apron tied around her waist. "It's so nice to finally meet you, Colton." She stuck out her hand, and when Colton's hand surrounded it, he worried he might break it as it was so small and fragile. Their height difference alone had to be more than a foot, making him feel like a giant.

Bowing his head, he said, "It's nice to meet you too, ma'am. It sure smells nice in here."

She smiled and turned back to the pan on the stove. "It's my grandmother's homemade spaghetti sauce, so I hope you're hungry." She pulled a loaf of garlic bread out of the oven and set it on the counter. When the noodles were drained, she placed a plate underneath and handed them to Colton. "Will you take this to the table, dear? It's just through this doorway." She followed him with the bread and set it down on the table.

Colton placed the bowl next to it and looked around, seeing that it was already set with four plates.

"How did you know I'd be coming to dinner?" he asked, confused.

The older woman smirked. "I've been married to this guy for over forty years. I've learned to be prepared. Besides, he called me before leaving the office."

Colton turned to the mayor. "You hadn't even asked me then."

"I may have had the perfect view to see Becca running out of the tree line and you following soon after. I figured you could use something to pick you up. Plus, you don't have to worry about running into her tonight." The mayor took his seat, and his wife swatted him on the side of the head.

"Be nice, Stan. You know that girl's been through a lot." She walked back into the kitchen and was gone a few moments.

Colton took a seat to the left of the mayor. He didn't want to ask any more about Becca, but their comments made him curious. "What happened to her? I asked her a few questions, and that's when she took off like a shot."

"Well, at least you got a good hug out of it. That's progress for our girl and a point in your favor, I'd think." The mayor leaned over, whispering while looking at the doorway. "She lost her parents and her brother. They were driving over to Salt Lake for her graduation from college in December five years ago. The car behind them slid right into their bumper, pushing the car off the road and down into a ravine. None of them survived."

Nothing had ever filled Colton with guilt as much as those words did. He couldn't imagine what it would be like to lose his entire family in one accident. No wonder college caused her to freeze. She was probably reliving the moments after she found out every time someone mentioned something about college or families.

"You didn't know, son. She blames herself for their deaths. I've heard her say a few times that she should've just stayed in Sage Creek and then they would all still be alive."

"But she doesn't know that. You can't ever know for certain."

Mayor Watkins gave him a sad smile. "Sometimes, it's easier to blame ourselves."

Dottie came back in with the pot of spaghetti sauce, causing the mayor to sit up straight in his seat. Colton tried not to laugh, but if the man was trying not to look suspicious about something, he was doing a horrible job.

"Should we say grace, dear?" the older man said.

"Not just yet. We're almost ready to eat." She glanced around the room and then left.

Colton glanced at the table of food. The large bowl of salad had already been there when he was asked to bring in the noodles. He was hungry, but he couldn't imagine the three of them would polish all this off.

He had to admit, it was fun seeing an older couple interact. All of his grandparents had passed on before he was born, and his father hadn't been in the picture for many years, which made his perception of relationships a bit skewed.

A knock came at the door, and when Dottie didn't answer it, the mayor called out, "Dottie, are you expecting company?" He stood and walked to the door, just out of eyesight from the table. There was some shuffling of feet, and Dottie came out of the kitchen just as Becca walked around the corner, only to stop dead in her tracks.

"Becca, I'm so glad you could come. There's so much pasta here, and I just knew you'd be able to help us eat it."

Becca's eyebrows turned down, accentuating the deep line in her forehead. She plastered on a smile and slid into the seat opposite Colton. She narrowed her eyes at him. "I didn't expect to see you here."

He shrugged. It wasn't his fault they'd both been invited. "The mayor saw me walking out his office window and figured I could use a warm welcome." He stared at her, enjoying her squirm. If she was thinking about the hug they'd shared, he was too, and a shiver ran up his spine.

Taking in a deep breath, he turned to the Watkins, hoping they were ready to eat so the sudden awkward tension could be over.

The mayor said grace, and the only sound at first was the clinking of dishes as the food was passed around the table. After a few bites, Colton was sick of the silence and looked around for something to talk about.

Pointing to the vase sitting in the middle of the table, he said, "What beautiful flowers. Did you get them from Becca's shop?"

The corner of Becca's mouth turned up just a bit as she turned the fork in her noodles, and Dottie grinned. "Stan forgot it was the forty-second anniversary of our first kiss the other day. I know it sounds ridiculous, but it's a good way for a girl to get flowers, don't you think?"

The tension dissolved, and the mayor grumbled about having to remember every date since the beginning of time.

"Oh, don't get your feathers ruffled, old man," Dottie said, hiding her mouth behind her hand as her shoulders shook. That got Becca laughing, and soon, Colton felt like he'd been through a decent ab workout.

After taking a few bites, Dottie leaned forward, her hands intertwined. "So, Colton, you're the one here to get the subdivision started, right?"

He nodded. "Yes, ma'am." He caught Becca scrunch her nose out of the corner of his eye but focused on Dottie.

"How long have you been a builder?"

"Twelve years. I've specialized mostly in finish work but have been working to move up in the company." He took a bite of bread, trying to distract his mind from retreating at the slew of personal questions coming his way. He'd never been one to go after attention, and he was already feeling the heat of invisible spotlights with the way Mrs. Watkins was looking at him.

Dottie gasped. "Twelve years? Dear, you don't look old enough to have been working for that long."

He glanced up at Becca, surprised to see her watching him, her eyes looking greener with the blouse she was wearing. Picking up his napkin, he wiped the sides of his mouth before looking in Dottie's direction.

"I started with the company just after turning eighteen. I began as the grunt man and then worked up to being a finish carpenter. This subdivision in your town would be my first chance to be a project manager."

Becca stiffened, and Colton knew that wasn't a good thing after only two days. Was there anything she wasn't sensitive to talking about? He wished there was some way to keep the fun, more relaxed side of her when he was around.

"What about your family, Colton? Do they live in Denver?" the mayor asked, twirling his fork in the spaghetti.

"Well, the short version is, my father left when I was really young, and my mother had major complications having me, so I'm an only child. She won't leave Boulder, but I'm hoping to move her closer to me soon."

Dottie reached over and patted his hand, much like he pictured a grandmother would.

"Is your mother all right?" Becca's voice caused him to turn in her direction, noting the tenderness with which she'd said the words. Now knowing about her family, he decided to tread carefully.

Colton shook his head. "She suffers from Alzheimer's. It's gotten so bad that she can't do much for herself anymore."

Becca rolled her lips in and gave him a sympathetic look. At least it was better than her running away from him.

The evening continued, and by the time dinner was

finished, Colton was sad to see it end. He'd never had a family meal like this and with such good conversation.

Dottie piled a large container of spaghetti and foil-wrapped garlic bread into his arms as he was leaving. "You can't eat out for every meal, and this way, all you need to do is warm it up. The hotel does have a microwave in your room, right? If not, I'll have to have a talk with Delia. People can't stay long in a place if they don't have a way to warm things up or cook them."

"It has a microwave," Colton said quickly, hoping she didn't go off on another long speech.

She gave him a small hug before turning to Becca and doing the same.

The mayor shook Colton's hand and winked. Leaning in, he whispered, "Don't screw it up."

No pressure.

Once the door closed, Becca looked at him and then took slow steps down the stairs to the front sidewalk. She stopped and turned so fast that Colton almost bumped into her.

"I'm sorry about earlier. I shouldn't have run away. There are a lot of things I'm trying to work through, and I'm not doing a very good job of it." She bit her bottom lip. "Do you mind if we start over?"

"Sounds good to me. But when I say something that bothers you, can you at least tell me what I said wrong so I don't keep doing it?" He tried to give her a serious face but softened when she smiled.

"Dani's right. I need to get over the past and start living for the day."

Colton's brain whirred, trying to figure out if he'd met Dani.

"Sorry, Dani's my best friend. She's in Europe right now, reporting for a news station and researching for her next book."

They were to the edge of the street now, and Colton stretched his leg forward, making sure the food didn't fall from the movement.

"You didn't want to go with her?" he asked.

She laughed, shaking her head like he'd come up with some hilarious joke. The sound was deep and refreshing, causing Colton to laugh along with her.

"Want and can't are different. But maybe someday I'll be over the fear of leaving this town."

Colton was speechless. "What do you mean?" He'd heard of people who couldn't bear to leave their homes, but someone who was fine around town but feared leaving it altogether—that was new.

Her face flushed, and he saw the signs of her clamming up again, so he rushed to say, "I'm sorry. I didn't mean it like that. I just hope your fear doesn't hold you back forever. Sage Creek is beautiful, but sometimes it's good to see other places. You'll appreciate the beauty of this place even more when you come back."

He saw the thoughts churning in her head and knew he'd better say good night before he said something to undo all the progress they'd made.

She took in a deep breath and nodded. "I'll get there. It just might take me longer than I want to get over my fears."

Colton nodded. Seeing the same vulnerability that had caused him to hug her earlier pulled at him again, but she stepped back as if sensing he was ready to move in.

"Well, I've got to go get some orders placed for work. It was good seeing you again." She gave a close-lipped smile and took another step back.

"I better get back to the hotel. I've got some emails to catch up on as well. Have a good night."

He walked slow, making sure she made it into her house before he disappeared down the street. As safe as Sage Creek seemed, he realized he didn't want anything else to add to the current fears Becca probably went through on a daily basis. The wall she'd originally put up seemed to be slowing dropping, and he hoped to still be here when it was down completely. Maybe then she'd finally trust him.

CHAPTER 10

*B*ecca woke up exhausted the next morning. After spending most of the night replaying the conversations at the Watkins, her curiosity was even more piqued about Colton. She'd nearly run from the house when she saw him sitting at the table, smelling some kind of scheme on the part of the older couple. But overall, it had been a good night with good food and even better company.

So far, she'd misjudged the builder, and when he talked about his mother, she could only imagine how hard it would be to still have her around but not have her mind be there all the time. The arrogance she'd thought she'd seen at the council meeting must have come more from nerves. She'd been surprised this would be his first job as a project manager. He'd said it once before, but she hadn't registered it until that conversation.

She wondered if he'd started working so young because of his mother's health. That was a big motivator for working instead of going to college. Peter had always boasted about how he'd scored the job he had because of his degree, but there was something about Colton staying with the same company for that long that proved his work ethic wasn't just in studying books.

She decided to make a trip down to where the proposed subdivision could be, knowing she needed to go at some point to fulfill her duty to the town council. The flower shop didn't normally open until later on Fridays, leaving her the whole morning free. Even with the wedding slated for the next morning, she was confident she could get everything done during the normal hours.

Becca pulled a brush through her hair, twisting several pieces so the curl would stay in from the day before. She pulled on a pair of jeans and a short-sleeved top, looking more casual than she did most days. With all the work ahead of her that afternoon, it would be better to be comfortable.

She walked out the door and grabbed her bike to roll slowly through the streets. The rays of the sun could be seen over the mountains, but the whole sphere hadn't come into view yet. There was something about the smell of the spring morning that held promise, and she made a mental note to do this more often.

That thought brought her back to the conversation on the Watkins's doorstep the night before. Colton's words about the world being beautiful and really appreciating what she had right here hit home. She knew there were some amazing things to see in the world. She just needed to get over her fears. Easier said, of course, as she'd been trying to figure out a way to venture out for over a year but still hadn't taken the plunge.

The ride to the proposed lots was over half a mile, but from the burn in her legs and the wheezing of her lungs, she knew she needed to get more exercise in every day.

Parking her bike at the side of the last building on Main Street, she pulled out a mini version of the proposed plans, trying to place how far apart the lots were and where the road into the subdivision would be located. All of which she hoped wouldn't happen, but she needed to be thorough if she was going to be able to dispute the construction company's claim.

Looking over the large field, she saw several discrepancies in the plans and knew those might be good ammo for the builder to have to at least redraw the plat map.

"Good morning. You're up early."

Colton's deep voice caused her to jump, sending a quick surge of adrenaline through her. "Did you sneak up on me?"

He shook his head. "No. I wasn't trying to be quiet. I think you were just too focused on that paper in your hands. What is that anyway?"

She pulled it to her chest, covering it with both hands. "Nothing. It's nothing."

The corner of his mouth turned up, and he reached a hand forward, lightly pulling at her wrist to see the paper. Again with the sparks from his touch. "It wouldn't happen to be a miniature map of the land now, would it?"

Becca tried to hide a grin and turned away, feeling the absence of his touch. "Maybe."

She was turned around completely, peeking over her shoulder to see where Colton stood. Using his height, he reached his long arm around her shoulder, his mouth near her ear. "Let me take a look at that." His fingers grabbed onto the paper and tugged upward with a little bit of force. Becca tried to hold on but gave up, letting him have it.

"Well, now that you're here with the contractor, what can I help you with? Do you have any questions about the property?"

"What are you planning on doing for water?" Becca leaned in to look at the map, her head lightly resting on his upper arm, sending her senses running out of control. Taking a step back, she swallowed once before looking him in the eye. "Do we have enough wells, or can the houses be hooked up to the town water without running everyone else dry?"

He wagged his finger at her. "That's a really good question, actually. We—"

"Wait. Did you think I wouldn't ask good questions?" She took a step toward him, both hands on her hips and her head tilted back enough to stare at him. She was baiting him, and the worried expression on his face made it hard to keep her own face neutral. He was cute when he was flustered.

He chuckled. "No. Not many people outside of contractors understand the importance of water systems. Because we have the lake up in the hills—"

"Pond," she cut in.

"Sorry, pond," he said, emphasizing it while smiling at her. "With the pond up there and Sage Creek running just on that side of the subdivision, those are options for an emergency. There are several natural springs running through the town that came up in the tests. The proposed lots would be using wells, unless the town allows for extra shares to hook into the town water system." He paused and glanced at her. "Was that too much?"

Becca shook her head. She liked that he didn't phrase it as a done deal just yet. Another part of her was in awe at how open he was about all of this. Peter had always kept things so hush-hush, making it hard to know when she could ask about something. Colton's face showed his excitement as he talked about it.

"Do you like your job?" she asked.

"I do. I mean, I know I can't be the carpenter forever, and overseeing a project is a new challenge I want to take on," Colton said, avoiding her gaze and stuffing one hand into his pant pocket. "I like seeing things put together. I can drive by several places in the suburbs of Denver and say, 'I worked on that house.'"

"That's cool." She'd never thought of building houses in that way, always thinking it was about the profit made and how quickly the job could be done. She paused a moment before turning around. "How big are the lots? I know they're a certain amount by looking at the plat map, but can you show me how big an acre is?"

Colton's face brightened as a smile spread across his face, and he leaned into her as he pointed to the stake to her right. "Sure. We have these stakes set here by the surveyors in the hopes that we will get this passed through." He pointed to a large rod right next to them and then signaled the ones positioned down the land. She was surprised at how big even a half-acre looked from this angle. Sure, it might not be the same with a house on it, but it was more property than most homes in town had.

She glanced around, unable to think of any more questions at the moment and trying to keep her mind from running back to the protective nature she felt when she was around Colton. Now, looking at the map, she realized things were fairly well drawn out. There went one of her reasons to dispute the whole thing. "Well, thank you for your help. I need to get back and open up the shop."

"Do you need a hand? I don't really have a lot to do until the council makes a decision." With his head tilted to the side and his smile emphasizing the scar on his chin, she was surprised at how much she wanted him to hang out a little more.

Coming to her senses, she shook her head. "I appreciate it, but I don't have any big orders today, and everything with the wedding is close to done, so it might be kind of boring for you."

Colton held up his hands and took his wallet out of his

back pocket. "No problem. Just let me know if you do need help." He pulled out a business card and handed it to her. "My cell is on there. Call or text."

Becca smiled and nodded. "Will do. Thank you."

He walked her back to her bike, strolling alongside her as she took the handlebars. They chatted about menial things as they moved along the road, Colton saying goodbye once they reached the hotel.

He waved to her before disappearing through the front door, and Becca couldn't get the imprint of his bright smile and chocolate-brown eyes out of her head all the way back to the flower shop.

CHAPTER 11

Going for a stroll down the street an hour or two later, Colton glanced at the shops as he passed them. He'd thought of this as a small town because it was nowhere near the size of Denver, but it wasn't like they had nothing. They had all the modern conveniences of a normal city, just in a more compact area.

The sign above the hardware store reminded him of Becca's words to include local businesses if the subdivision was passed. He stepped through the door and browsed the shelves, looking at the gleaming tools and random gadgets stocked there.

Someone stopped him and asked, "Can I help you with something?"

Colton shook his head. "No, I'm just checking out what you've got here."

The young man pointed at him. "You must be that new contractor, right?"

When Colton nodded his head, the man smiled, holding out his hand to shake, which Colton did. "I hope when the subdivision gets approved, you'll look at using some of the supplies I have here. I know sometimes it's cheaper to ship from the bigger cities, but us little guys can always use a little leg up, you know? And I have several contacts to be able to order in bulk and get a great price."

That was something Colton could get behind. "When I get all the information, I'll give you a list to bid, and we'll go from there. If I can use things locally, I'd prefer that."

The man's face lit up. "I'm Tanner Hart. What was your name?"

"Colton Maxfield. To be honest, this would be my first time being a project manager. I'm just hoping the town council passes it." He let out a strangled laugh, realizing how much work this kind of building would be. He'd only ever worked on one home at a time, and arranging the subcontractors for each phase of building for several projects at once would definitely be a challenge.

"Me too. Well, it's great to meet you. I'm the owner of this shop as of three months ago when my father decided to retire, so I'd like to get some more work going and get this place built up."

There was nothing Colton liked better than working with people of the same mind. And working locally sometimes had its advantages.

A customer came in, and Tanner moved away, helping the man at the front desk.

Colton walked even slower through the aisles, picking up nails and screws, trying not to think about how bored he was without work. By the time he made it up to the front desk, the man Tanner had left to help was there with several supplies.

"I don't know how I'm going to get this done," the man was saying to Tanner. "I don't have much knowledge in building, but my wife thinks I do. And my budget tells me we can't hire anyone right now." He looked to be in his late 60s or early 70s.

Stepping forward, Colton asked, "What is it you're working on?"

The man turned around and shook his head. "My wife's been watching those home renovation shows and thinks she needs more character in our living room."

"Let me guess…she wants more shiplap?" Colton said with a smile.

"Do you know what that is?" the man asked.

When Colton nodded, he continued, "I had to ask her, and she made me watch one of her shows. These new terms. I was an accountant for years, but when it comes to building stuff, I'm lost."

"Well, I'm a contractor, and I have some free time. I can come along and help you."

"You would do that? I can give you a little bit of money, but I don't have much more in the budget this month for it."

Colton waved him off. It wasn't like this was a complete remodel, and it might help pass the time until more people were out and about or off work. "Don't worry about it. You can just think of it as a service for helping this bored guy to stay out of trouble."

"I like your way of thinking." The man grinned, tapping his pointer finger against the side of his head and directing it at Colton. "If you'll grab the tools, son, we'll get going. Don't want to burn too much daylight."

Colton picked up the tools on the counter, and Tanner motioned for them to meet around back in the lumber yard. After pulling out several one-by-six pieces of lumber, they loaded them into the man's well-kept but dated Ford.

"Hop in, kid. We just live a few streets up."

Colton smiled and slid in. He hadn't been called kid in quite a while. "What was your name, sir?"

"Gordon McCready. And yours?"

When Colton told him, he smiled and nodded, maneuvering the truck through the narrow lumber yard and out onto the street. "You're the one who's supposed to build a bunch of homes, right?"

Nodding, Colton chuckled a bit. "Yes, that's what brought me to your town. Are you for or against the new subdivision going in?"

Mr. McCready smiled. "Honestly, I'm so old it wouldn't really matter to me. But there are a lot of us older folks, and if we don't get some new blood in soon, it will be tough on the younger ones. A bunch of them are already having to cover several things at once, so I'd say I'm for it."

A jolt of hope shot through Colton's chest. He was starting to see that maybe he wasn't doomed at getting the right signatures. Maybe more people in Sage Creek realized how critical it was for new development.

As they drove up the road, he thought about the conversation he'd had with Becca that morning. She'd seemed determined to figure out a way to derail the whole thing, but by the time she left him at the hotel, he'd gotten the feeling she was starting to give in to the idea.

They pulled into the driveway of a small home, the outside a faded sage-green trimmed in white.

"How long have you lived here?" Colton asked, unbuckling his seat belt.

"Over forty years, son. It's still standing after five sons and one daughter, so I think if I can make it through a few more years of my wife's remodeling ideas, it will have survived just about every phase of our married life." The man chuckled as he slid out of the truck.

Walking into the McCready home, Mr. McCready introduced Colton to his wife, and she grinned.

"Gordon thinks I'm the craziest person ever, but I just

love the style of that one gal. Everything she does just turns out gorgeous. I figured a little sprucing up wouldn't be bad for our little cottage."

Colton smiled and nodded, waiting for her to explain her vision. Life was always easier when he listened to what a client wanted first before trying to get things put together.

Several hours later, Colton stood back to admire the work. It would still need to be painted, but he'd gotten all the wood hung.

Mrs. McCready brought him in a glass of lemonade, and he was grateful for her kindness. She'd brought him lunch earlier and had given him several compliments throughout the day of work.

"Oh my goodness! This looks amazing. Now with a little paint, it will just finish off this room." She clapped her hands together, close to bouncing on her feet.

"You'll probably want to caulk the edges before you paint. That way, it'll give you a smoother finish." Colton walked forward and pointed to the small gaps.

"We appreciate all your work, son. Take this." The man reached out his hand and tried to give Colton some money.

Taking a step back, Colton raised his hands and shook his head. "Oh, no, no. I can't take your money. You just saved me a day of boredom in the hotel room, plus lunch." He looked back at the wall and ran his hand over some of the boards. "This was a lot of fun, too. I haven't been able to do specialty pieces like this in quite some time. So, thank you."

"Are you sure, hun?" Mrs. McCready asked with a serious look. "You did a lot of work here for us today."

"No. Like I said, it was good for me. If you need some help with that painting, let me know. I just might have a few more empty boring days ahead of me while I'm here."

Mr. McCready slapped him on the back. "Of course, kid. It's nice when someone else is willing to do the work for me."

The old man grinned while his wife elbowed him in the side, causing him to double over.

Checking his watch, Colton saw it was near five. He wasn't sure what he should be doing, but his thoughts went to Becca. He wondered if she'd closed up shop already. With a grin, he said, "Mr. McCready, you should use that money to buy your wife some flowers."

Mrs. McCready held on to Colton's arm. "Oh my! You're quite the catch. Are you married? Do you have a girlfriend?"

And with that, he was ready to go. When those questions started popping up, he knew he was destined for a blind date if he didn't tread carefully. "No, ma'am. I'm not attached, but I've really got to get going. Have a great night, and I'll see you around."

Once down the steps, he took a few strides and then jogged, hoping Mrs. McCready wouldn't chase him down until he gave her all the details of his personal life. He turned south at Main Street and knew where he was. That was another great thing about a small town. He didn't get all turned around like in Denver.

Sticking his hands in his pockets, he walked by the flower shop, seeing a light on and several people inside. A sudden anxiety filled him as he realized how much he wanted to see Becca again.

After pausing for a few seconds of internal debate about whether or not she'd be weirded out that he popped in again, he walked to the front door of the shop and opened it, feeling the air conditioning versus the balmy weather outside. There were at least ten people milling about the front section, some of them sitting on the chairs in the room while others looked into the coolers placed along the wall or stared blankly at their phones.

Becca came out with two boxes and a small bouquet of

white flowers, her face flushed and the hair on the side of her head splaying out like a small halo.

"Mr. Perkins, here are your two orders. One dozen long-stemmed roses and another of lilies." She tapped a few keys on the cash register and looked up at him. "Forty-five twenty-one."

The man stepped forward with a card stretched out, and Becca took it, swiping it with ease. Once the transaction was done, she scanned the room, her eyes resting on Colton for just a moment. A quick smile graced her features before she searched the room again.

"Sally, here is your bouquet."

After the transaction was over, Colton took several steps forward. "Are you all right? I don't think I've ever seen this many people in a flower shop, even in a big city like Denver."

Becca groaned and walked through the swinging door to the back room. Colton thought about it and then followed her in.

"The truck that was supposed to be here when I opened at eleven was delayed, meaning all the orders from today couldn't be put together until it got here. I've been scrambling to get it all done, and my one employee just left to go to some overnight activity for school."

Colton stood next to her at the long table, watching her work with the flowers. "Put me to work. Do you have another apron?" He usually wouldn't mind trimming flowers and doing whatever she needed without it, but he could feel the sawdust clinging to him from a day of working with wood, and he didn't want to ruin the flowers.

She pointed to the wall near the door to the front, never taking her eyes away from the several flowers she'd already placed in the large vase.

He tied the strings around his waist and walked to stand

next to her again. "I guess at least the truck made it. Otherwise, you'd have some unhappy customers."

Becca squinted, and her jaw moved to one side as she rearranged a couple of the flowers. "That's actually a good point. I've been over here fuming because of the delay, but with all the orders set to go out tonight and the wedding in the morning, it would have been tough to pay the rent this month without them."

"I'm sure it would be hard letting the people of this town down. You seem to care about them all a lot." Colton picked up the scissors and started trimming some of the stems in the piles surrounding the bouquet. At least he could help somewhat, even if he didn't have an eye for colors. For wood and making a clean cut, he was almost a master. Flowers, not so much.

She nodded and glanced in his direction, her eyes sad. "I owe them all a lot. They came together to help me when I was at my lowest of lows. Twice, even. There are so many people here who I consider a surrogate parent or grandparent because they've always taken an interest in my life. That saying about a village raising a child? I think it applies to adults too."

Colton nodded, surprised by the revelation. He knew how hard it must have been to have her parents die, but what would have been her second low? A girl with as much fire and grit as Becca made it hard for him to picture her as having a hard time with anything long term.

"There are several boxes of flowers over there near the side door. Will you bring a few of them over so I can sort through the ones that need to go out now?" She moved the vase over to the ribbon section and pulled out a bright blue one, measuring it against her arm.

Grateful to be of use, Colton jumped into action and grabbed the boxes, setting them next to the table. Becca had disappeared with the vase but was back on his next return with a box, already cutting into the one he'd brought over.

Sensing her need to concentrate, he stayed quiet and did the best he could to help, wondering if he was hindering more than anything. Over an hour later, Becca came in, tucking the loose strands of hair behind her ears, and sat down in one of the chairs.

"Are we all done for the night?" Colton asked, wondering about the ten other boxes he'd pulled over.

She gave him a weak smile. "I wish. Thank you for your help. That rush was a doozy. You can head out if you need to. I know you probably have something fun to do."

Colton laughed out loud, and Becca narrowed her eyes at him. "I do. I'd say working with flowers is fun."

"I think so, but I'm not so sure about you." Becca's grin brightened her already attractive features, and he had to pull his gaze away from her.

"If you still have work to do, I'm here to help. I'm sure it will go faster with one pair of competent hands and a gopher, right?" He twisted his lips to the side, and she laughed louder than he'd heard since he got to town.

"This isn't some ploy to get me to agree to the subdivision, is it?" Becca's smile faded, and she looked at him out of the corner of her eyes, as if sizing up his true intentions.

Hands raised, Colton said, "Not at all. My mother taught me to help those in need, and I'd say you're in need right now."

"Well, then I'll have to thank your mom. Let's get started."

CHAPTER 12

*B*ecca was surprised at how fast Colton learned. He might not be the best at tying a bow around a bouquet or a box, but he'd already memorized several of the flowers they'd worked with over the past hour and had definitely cut the time it would take to get everything ready in half.

The panic she'd felt as the hours ticked by while waiting for the truck had slowly ebbed away as she worked next to him, catching the musky scent of his cologne every once in a while. He was funny and quick-witted, his quips causing her to laugh more than once. She appreciated the company, even if she was still a bit leery of his intentions. If he was trying to persuade her to vote for the subdivision, he was going all out for it.

With all the flowers arranged or prepped for the next morning, Becca blew out a long breath.

"I can't thank you enough for your help tonight," she said, smiling at Colton.

"No problem. I feel more useful than if I'd gone back to

the hotel and watched TV for the duration of the evening." He grinned, and she saw the scar on his chin again.

She reached up and touched the spot but pulled her hand back as she realized he was watching her, the corner of his mouth turned up. His eyes stared into hers, making her knees buckle. At least she was already next to the table.

"Sorry. I just noticed you had a scar there. What happened?"

"When I was a kid, I loved climbing trees. My mother got to the point that when she was looking for me, she'd go outside and look in every tree in our yard. One time I was trying to climb up too fast and didn't see a broken branch. It sliced pretty deep, but we didn't have good insurance, so my mom put a bandage over it."

"No stitches, huh?"

Colton shook his head. "No, she watched it, though. She'd clean it out every day with hydrogen peroxide and bandage it up. I got a lot of scrapes over the years, and she probably saved us quite a bit by being an at-home nurse."

Something about his words caused Becca's heart to swell. Her parents had always been middle class, and she'd never truly wanted for any of the necessities. But she'd never really thought of things like insurance as being something to go without. A doctor visit in town was just a normal thing, but then again, she hadn't really needed to get checked out in the past few years, even though Danielle kept pestering her about therapy.

"How about a milkshake? The diner is open late on Fridays, and I owe you for staying so long to help me." She patted the table with her hand as she waited for his response.

"Sounds good, but I'll buy."

Shaking her head and her pointer finger in front of him, she said, "I don't think so, Mr. Builder. Like I said, I owe you."

Becca grabbed her purse and turned off the lights before

moving out the side door. The diner wasn't too far, but the sky distracted her. Its blue-black shone against the large nearly-full moon and the spattering of stars. She'd been back here for several years, but she hadn't taken much time to enjoy it all since she'd come back after graduation, like she'd put herself into a tunnel of the places she had to go and never glanced at the rest of it. She'd never been able to see the sky as clearly when she'd gone to college. This view was just one of the many reasons she didn't want to leave this small town.

"Last night you said your mother wouldn't leave Boulder. Did you grow up in the Denver area?" Becca asked, breaking the comfortable silence between them.

"On the outskirts. We moved to a couple of suburbs throughout the years, but I moved into the city once I graduated high school. Work was more consistent there, and with my mom's health, we needed something more steady. She wouldn't come, though. Said the dirty city air would only make her symptoms worse."

Becca thought about that and then asked, "And your father?"

"Gone by the time I was three. He was a pilot, so it wasn't like I noticed a whole lot when he was finally gone. He'd leave for two or three weeks at a time and then only be home for a couple of days before taking off again. Then one time, he just didn't come back. My mom never really said much about it until I asked her in high school. He'd found a new life somewhere else, and we weren't a part of it."

Feeling like she'd just been punched in the gut, Becca reached over, touching his arm lightly. "I'm so sorry, Colton. I can't even imagine."

He shrugged. "It was a long time ago. There are a lot of things I would have liked to ask him, but then again, I made it this far. My mom worked at one of the local restaurants for years until she couldn't hold up the trays anymore. At that point, I was already working wherever I could."

Becca let out a nervous laugh. "I feel somewhat guilty now. My parents let me do what I wanted as long as I wasn't causing trouble. I didn't have to think about a job, even in college." For some reason, even mentioning college didn't have the same bite it had before he'd come to town. "But I've found that working has a way of soothing some of the times when I could go crazy. So you graduated high school and started working for Dream Homes?"

He bobbed his head back and forth, looking indecisive. "Kind of, yeah. Dream Homes is a smaller company under Summers Construction. They primarily built commercial buildings, but my old boss wanted to get into the residential sector, thinking it would be a good way to diversify. His son, my new boss, Adam, just took over for his dad a few months ago with this section, and as much as I want this deal to work out, he's more cutthroat than I am."

"What do you mean by that?" A pit formed in her stomach as her nerves reacted to his comments.

"I mean that he doesn't look at the overall situation. It's the dollar signs he's worried about and how fast we can make them. His father is a lot different, someone I always felt I could confide in and be straight with. Adam is kind of a stereotypical spoiled rich kid who has the job he has because of his family."

Becca nodded. She'd met several of those kinds of people in school. It hadn't taken long for her to learn who the influential families of Salt Lake were, especially when those students were in her classes. Not all were privileged and snotty, but there were more than she'd imagined.

"So, you're not completely convinced about this subdivision, then?" She heard the hope in her voice and wished she could rephrase it without looking like an idiot.

He chuckled as he opened the door to the diner. "No, the subdivision is something I think this town needs. Not all apartments bring the bad sort; believe me. Sometimes people just need the chance to get back on their feet with affordable housing while not feeling like they've been put out with the trash."

Becca thought about his words, wondering if they struck home more than she expected. But seeing it from that perspective made her realize how much she'd truly been given.

As they took a seat at the bar, Velda wiggled her eyebrows at Becca as Colton settled in. The older woman turned to Colton. "We didn't run you out of town yet, huh?"

"No, ma'am. Not yet." He smiled wide at her. "I figured I'd stick around and see what the small-town life is like."

"And how's that working out for you?"

Becca shifted in her seat, turning to face him as she waited for his response.

He nodded a few times, glancing at Becca once before looking in Velda's direction again. "I'm a fan of this town. Everyone I've met has been really accommodating."

Velda turned and pointed to Becca. "Are you sure she's been that way?"

Colton looked in Becca's direction and smiled, his teeth shining through. It made his whole face light up, and Becca averted her eyes, feeling a little self-conscious.

"She's gone above and beyond to make me feel at home here."

Becca's head shot up, eyes wide at his statement. She hadn't been the most congenial person when he'd come to town, and she'd even run away from him after he tried to console her.

"That's what I like to hear," Velda said, winking at Becca once again.

Needing to get this conversation on another track, Becca said, "Can I get the usual?" before pushing her menu back to the woman. She was more hungry than she'd expected, realizing she hadn't stopped for lunch or dinner.

"Are you still cold, honey? I can switch the hot chocolate for a soda or something. You know it's almost summertime, right?"

"There's just something about hot chocolate that makes me—" She stopped, seeing Colton's eyes searching her face. What she wanted to say was that hot chocolate reminded her of her parents and the many times they'd sat around the dinner table, sipping from their mugs and chatting about anything under the sun, the easy stuff and the deeper, tougher issues. But after the nearly carefree day she'd had, she didn't want to spoil it with tears.

An idea popped into her head, the design of Velda's hair clip inspiring her. She pulled out a pen from her purse and started drawing on the napkin in front of her.

"That's a cool design. Do you draw when you're bored?" he asked, leaning over a few inches.

Her eyes went wide, and both her hands flew to the page, covering the swirls. After a minute, she sighed and removed her hands. "Sometimes I get inspiration in the weirdest places. I have to hurry and sketch it out or else I forget about it. This is going to be a pendant."

"Do you create a lot of jewelry?"

She shrugged. "I guess it depends. I just like to make sure I use the flowers that don't get sold, and there are a lot of possibilities with all the different colors. I use the petals for different sections and then use wire for the rest."

"Sorry, I'm having a hard time picturing the petals not wilting."

"I use resin to cover them, keeping the bright colors from fading or turning brown." She finished off the small design with a few more strokes. "I have a small table at the front of my shop where I display them."

Colton rested his hand in his palm, his body turned to her directly. "What inspired you this time?"

"I do believe that is a very personal question, Colton Maxfield." She raised her chin and gave him a hint of a smile. "Maybe I can share that stuff with you when we've known each other longer than two days."

Colton raised an eyebrow. "So, you're hoping to know me longer than that?" He gave her a cockeyed grin.

She scowled. "That's not what I meant. I'm just saying we've known each other for a couple of days. I'm not usually an open book." She went back to sketching, making sure to get it as close to the picture in her mind as she could.

Velda came over with a soda for Colton and Becca's hot chocolate. "Don't let her kid you, Colton. She can talk your ear off when she wants to."

"Good to know." Colton's mischievous smile disappeared as he took a sip of his beverage out of the straw.

Becca flashed Velda a grimace, but the woman winked, her smile signaling she was up to something. Becca could only imagine.

She and Colton chatted about easy things as they ate their food. Once it was gone, Becca ordered them both a milkshake, making sure the woman knew the tab would go to her. It was the least she could do to repay the man after all his help. Plus, she felt like it was less like a date if she paid. At least, that's what she was telling herself.

The more time they spent together, the more comfortable she was with him. If she let things continue, she'd end up with a broken heart one way or another. He'd either leave town or realize the same thing Peter had before he broke off their engagement. Becca wasn't worth loving.

CHAPTER 13

After the milkshake, Colton managed to get Velda to charge the food to his card without Becca knowing, which he counted as a win.

He and Becca walked out the door, and Colton wasn't ready to head back to the hotel. "Is there a place you like to go to think?"

Becca turned and looked at him, the glassiness of her eyes under the moonlight only heightening the attraction he'd felt building throughout the day.

She nodded, and they walked in silence toward Town Hall, stopping in front of the large water fountain. The water flew up out of the top and spilled over the edges of the different tiers, the lighting on each making the whole thing dance before him.

"So, what's the story with this spot? Why do you like to come here?"

She sat on the bench and stared at the fountain in a trance. "My father started the fundraiser to get it put in after the deaths of the students. He used to bring us here all the time, me and my brother. We would play with the birds that hung around, and he'd give us coins to throw into the fountain for a wish."

"Did any of those wishes come true?" His question stopped her short, and she glanced up at him, her eyes unfocused like she didn't really see him.

"I'm not sure. I can't remember any of them."

Colton leaned forward and reached into his pants pocket to pull out two coins. He moved to sit on the bench with Becca, handing her a coin. "Throw it in. Even though we're not kids anymore, we can still dream." He could feel her eyes on him as he closed his own, searching his heart for his wish. His first thought was to know what it was like to kiss Becca Taylor. He opened his eyes and tossed the coin into the fountain, smiling as he did so.

He turned and stared at her, seeing the indecision in her face. "Just play along. Sometimes we give up on our dreams as adults when what we should be doing is going out and getting them."

She raised one eyebrow and seemed to be trying not to smile. "So, you're chasing all your dreams?"

Colton shifted back against the bench, turning his focus back to the fountain. He bit the inside of his mouth as he debated what to tell her. "Not all, but a few. What about you?"

She paused a moment. "No, I guess not."

Making her wish, she kissed the coin and tossed it into the fountain. If only he could have been the coin right then.

"Does kissing it help the wish come true?" Colton asked, his stomach flipping when she beamed.

"I don't know. I guess we'll find out."

Sitting there on the bench, it wasn't long before a chill wind came around, probably from the pond up the trail from them. He glanced over and saw Becca's lower lip quiver, and her teeth chattered together as she rubbed her hands up and down her bare arms.

Taking a chance, he scooted closer and draped his arm around her. "It's colder here than Denver. I should have thought to bring a jacket."

Becca's body was stiff for several seconds, and Colton almost let go, but then she relaxed against him. "I'm the one who should know better. The wind coming down from the canyon can be brutal." She turned her head slightly, but not enough to completely face him. The corner of her mouth moved up a fraction of an inch, and then it was gone, her focus back on the fountain in front of them.

Colton glanced up at the stars, breathing out deeply. He'd never imagined he'd have feelings for someone like the ones that were snowballing out of control inside him for the girl at his side. Long ago, he'd told himself that if he couldn't be at home for longer than a couple of weeks at a time, it wasn't worth trying to settle down. He didn't want to abandon his mother like his dad had done, didn't want to have that guilt when he came through the door that his kids would barely know him.

And up until now, he'd been happy. He had a good job and was able to support his mother, all the while living like a bachelor in the city. But in just a few days, he'd been shown that there was a significant piece of his life he was missing out on. Maybe there was a chance here.

Just as quickly as the flicker of hope entered his chest, he shook it off.

"So, what else do you like to do around here?" Colton asked, breaking through his thoughts. If things with the city council passed, he'd be the source of hurt for Becca, taking away some of the stability she'd come to lean on over the years since her parents' accident.

"Uh, that's a good question. I usually—"

"Oh, good. Becca, there you are. Do you have time to help me with the decorations for the Founder's Day Festival?" The woman who'd introduced herself as Susie before the subdivision meeting stood to Becca's right, trying to send Colton vibes he wasn't feeling. She reminded him too much of the women who hung around Adam at the company parties, and Colton didn't want to give any indication of interest.

"You'll be fine. Just let me know what flowers you need, and we'll go from there. Don't you need to be setting up for the wedding tomorrow?" Becca's tone came out irritated, and as much as Colton tried to read what was going on between the two of them, he couldn't figure out their relationship.

"Larissa only bought her dress from me. Her mom hired some out-of-town designer, so I'm trying to get a jump start on the festival."

Becca nodded, turning her attention back to the fountain.

Something about this interaction was off as Becca's figure grew stiff against the back of the bench. But maybe Colton didn't know her well enough yet to figure it all out.

SHE'D SAT on the bench, trying to figure out what to wish for. It had been so long since she'd hoped for anything for herself, mostly just that things wouldn't change from the easy-going pace it had been for the last few months. Knowing herself, she'd finally wished that she could be happy no matter what changed in the next few months.

Of all the times Susie could pop up, why did it have to be right now? The night had been close to magical, and while Becca wasn't sure she trusted all the emotions flowing through her, she'd had a feeling that Colton was starting to like her a bit.

As much as she tried to tamp down those feelings, a

giddiness flowed through her. He'd pulled her closer, helping her warm up a bit against the wind. Maybe she should have said she needed to get home since it was getting late and colder. But she found she wanted whatever it was she was feeling to last a bit longer.

Now, with Susie standing there in her perfect outfit and runway-ready hairstyle, Becca realized her chances were slim. Susie had admitted the other day how she had her eye on the stranger, and Becca was bound to come out on the losing end. Not that she was bad-looking, but flirting wasn't something she was a master at.

Susie had taken over the assignment of directing the Founder's Day Festival this year, giving Becca a break after the last four years. Becca was grateful for the extra time. Or, she had been until Mr. Carpenter came to town.

Susie shook her head. "No, seriously, we're in trouble. I'll admit it. There's a lot of pressure since you pulled it off without a hitch for so long. Can you please just give me your opinion on a few things? Your eye for placement and style is flawless."

Heat brushed up Becca's neck, and she made sure to avoid eye contact with Colton. Being good at things outside of making money had been something Peter thought was a waste of time. He'd enjoyed it the first year he'd come to the festival, but once he got his job with the big construction company in Denver, all he ever talked about was work. Was that when he'd begun to change? With the new job?

Shaking her head, Becca knew now was not the time to dissect her past relationship.

"I don't know what I can do to help, Susie. You have some great skills for planning events too. I mean, you plan weddings. Those are way more intense than the town festival." Becca was surprised the words came out of her mouth, but she realized they were true. Susie had a natural flair for things that came easily enough for Becca, but she was able to capitalize on it enough to create a wonderland.

Susie bent over and grabbed her wrist, pulling her to a standing position. "Just indulge me, please. I know how big of a deal this is to the town, and I don't want to ruin it. I need someone to bounce ideas off of, and Marcy Baker hasn't shown up once." The girl stuck out her bottom lip and clasped her hands together.

"Okay, fine. I'll help you. Just stop whining." Becca nodded in Colton's direction, mostly to politely say goodbye.

"I can come help too if you need." Colton's voice floated over Becca's shoulder, and she turned and gave him a look of exasperation. If he thought he was helping, he wasn't. This was probably exactly what Susie had hoped for, that he'd tag along and fall for her charms.

But then again, maybe it would be better for him to spend time with Susie. Then Becca could seal her heart back up and not worry about falling for the wrong guy once again. The one who'd tell her everything she wanted to hear, only to leave her humiliated in front of the entire town.

"Perfect!" Susie cried, fluttering her long eyelashes a bit more than normal. "The more the merrier."

The Community Rec Building was only a block away, but Susie kept pulling on Becca's arm so hard she felt as if they were sprinting to get there. Colton just chuckled as he strolled next to her, hands in his pockets and looking more than attractive at the moment. Becca whipped her head around to make sure he wasn't in her peripheral anymore, hoping to quell her thoughts by focusing on the decorations.

They walked inside, and Becca was surprised to find it so empty. "Have you checked on all the decorations in the shed? I made sure we had each box labeled and put together on the shelves to make it easier to find this year."

"There's a shed for your town festival decorations?" Colton's eyebrow lifted like she was crazy.

"You laugh now, but just wait until you see what we're in for. If you're here long enough for the festival, that is." Becca couldn't help but tap him on the chest with the back of her hand. The hardness of his chest caused her to bite her lower lip. She should probably make a rule to avoid touching him at all costs if she was going to keep from being hurt.

"When's the festival?" he asked, crossing his arms over his chest, making his muscles stand out even more.

Becca shook her head. "It's, uh, in two weeks."

"I might just have to extend my stay no matter what the vote is. I'm curious to see what all the hype is about for this festival."

A group of butterflies took off in Becca's stomach, and all she could do was smile and turn away. She shouldn't be excited at that thought. What she needed was for him to go so she could walk around the town in peace, not having to guard her heart against the numberless charms and good qualities he had.

Becca knew how excited people got for the festival, and it was one reason she was relieved not to have to worry about it this year. There were several paintings and sculptures displayed every year as tradition for some reason or another. Every once in a while, a few new pieces were put up, but for the most part, it was up to the planner and her committee to decorate the cultural hall.

"Okay, Susie. What are you thinking?"

Susie's eyes went wide, and she bit her nail, looking around the room. "I was thinking we can have a big time frame set aside for singing and acting. I know we always have the town choir sing in the evening, but why not have some slots earlier to allow people to do a solo or sing with a group? There are several good actors and readers, and I thought we'd give them the chance to display those talents."

Becca's initial reaction was no, seeing as how they hadn't done that kind of thing in the past. But a few people popped into her mind, and she knew they would love this opportunity. "I think that would be really fun. Where are you planning to put the food?"

The girl moved into action, walking to the middle of the room. "I was thinking about putting up folding walls or something to divide the room here in the middle. There would be an opening so people can still hear the performances, but that way, the tables won't be scattered throughout the entire hall. The food will be over at the far end, near the kitchen, and the displays will be against the wall."

All of it sounded pretty good to Becca, and she wished she'd thought of it in years past.

"The biggest change I want to make is that once dinner is over, we'll have people gather up the chairs in front of the stage so we can have a dance."

Swallowing hard, Becca squeaked out, "A dance?"

"Yes, I think it would be so fun. After playing all day with the parade and events, we could have a dance for the adults."

"What about the kids?" Colton's words caused Becca to turn toward him, surprised he voiced the same thing she was about to.

Susie smiled. "I've already talked to some of the younger teenage girls, and they'd be hanging out with the kids in the large rooms upstairs. Adults can have a night out and not have to worry about babysitting."

Becca laughed. "Girl, I don't know what you needed me for. It sounds like you've got the night covered."

"You think it will be okay?" The insecurity in the woman's eyes caused Becca's heart to soften toward her somewhat.

Reaching out a hand, she placed it on Susie's shoulder. "I think it'll be great. Keeping traditions from the past and starting some fun new ones. The town will love it."

Seeing movement out of the corner of her eye, Becca turned and saw Colton at the door. "Where are you going?"

"I've got to take this call, but I'll head over to Tanner's store and pick up some stuff tomorrow to make the bifold walls, unless you've already got them stashed in that shed of yours."

Susie clapped her hands together. "Oh, that would be perfect. I hadn't quite figured out that part yet."

Becca frowned. "Wait, you know Tanner?"

Colton turned to look at her and gave her a half-smile. "I'm a builder. The hardware store is to me as the mall is to most girls." He winked before walking out the door.

Becca stood there, stunned, staring at the door as if he would come back in at any moment. Why couldn't the somersaults in her stomach stop? When he'd said he was trying to get to know people in town, she'd thought it was some line to get her to trust him. Maybe there was something a little different about him than she'd originally thought. She wished it didn't interest her as much as it did, and the differences between Colton and Peter seemed to diverge more and more every time she and Colton were together.

Wrapping one arm around Susie, Becca said, "I think this will be our best year yet, Susie. Are there some decorations you need to create in the next week or two?"

Susie smiled and stared at the door. "Yes, most of it is in the back conference room. He's a looker, isn't he?"

It took a moment for Becca to make the jump from decorations back to Colton. Her ears burned, and she licked her lips, hoping to bring back some of the moisture. "If you like that type of guy, yeah, I guess he is."

"What are you talking about? Besides a few changes in his face, he's basically the body double for Peter."

Becca winced and turned, pretending to pick up a piece of paper from the ground. She'd hoped everyone had forgotten about Peter, even though she tortured herself almost daily with thoughts of him, the what-might-have-beens and what she would have changed had she seen the signs sooner. But at least she hadn't wasted her life married to the guy. At least he'd saved her from that.

Turning around, Becca lifted her chin a bit. "Maybe my taste in men has changed. I'm going for blonds now."

Susie scrunched her face like she didn't quite believe her, but she didn't say anything more, for which Becca was grateful.

Appearance-wise, Susie had hit it on the head. Body type and hair color, even eye color, were the same. Colton's nose wasn't as sharp as Peter's, and his jaw looked more firm.

Just another reason to avoid him as much as possible. Getting involved with a guy like that would only end up with her heart in pieces again.

CHAPTER 14

Tanner knew exactly what they needed when Colton explained the concept Saturday afternoon. He'd tried to get an early start, but it seemed the only thing that stayed open during a town event like a wedding was the grocery store.

"That'll be a nice change," Tanner said. "Becca made some good changes when she first took over, but the town can't handle too many at once, especially with a time-honored tradition like the Founder's Day Festival."

Curious, Colton asked, "What did Becca change about it?"

"Everything, if you think back over the four years since she took it over. We used to play Bingo and have a two-hour program about the founding of Sage Creek. She was able to condense it down to a ten-minute program and then made it so we have raffles and other contests. My favorite is the pie contest. If you can be a judge of that, you'll be in heaven."

With a grin, Colton nodded. There hadn't been many pies he didn't like.

He took the bag Tanner handed him, waving goodbye as he walked out of the hardware store. He drove his truck around back where he loaded the pieces of wood he would need to create the bifold walls.

When he arrived at the center, he unloaded the supplies, bringing them into the building and leaning them to one side. He heard talking and moved to the doorway on the far wall, finding the girls tangled up in tulle and ribbon.

"Oh, you were so fast!" Susie said, batting her eyes at him. He had to hold in a laugh as her eyelashes looked more like a butterfly flapping its wings than anything attractive to him.

"I think I have all the supplies needed for the bifold walls. When do you need them done by?"

"Before the festival in two weeks. Will you have time to finish them before you leave us?"

With a nod, he said, "They won't be too hard to build. I'm not the best painter in the world, so if you want something other than the color of those boards out there, you'll have to figure that one out yourself."

"That should be fine. One less thing on the list if I don't have to paint." Susie laughed, tying a piece of ribbon around a large section of tulle. "You don't have to work on them tonight. It's already late afternoon."

Becca walked into the large room, pieces of fabric slung over her shoulder and something else in her hand. When she saw him, she gave him a warm smile. "I didn't see you at the wedding this morning. Did you do anything fun?" She looked back at the fabric in her hand, pulling a needle and thread through it.

She took a seat at the table where Susie was working, pulling the fabric a bit tighter to make a ruffle. Unfolding a chair against the wall, Colton took a seat at the table, watching as Becca's fingers moved with ease. "I took a little hike behind the pond. It's beautiful up there. Is there something I can do to help you two?" he asked, looking between the women.

Susie smiled. "Sit there and talk to us. What do you like to do besides building back in Denver?"

Colton wasn't sure what to say. His life had become building, and since he didn't have any family close, he didn't feel guilty about working late. Until he arrived in Sage Creek, that is. It seemed like he should have ten extracurricular activities, or so the people had commented.

"Not much. In the winter, I coach junior hockey for one of the clubs there."

"You must be so good with kids. I wouldn't know the first thing to say to them. I'm not good at motivational speaking." Susie stroked her hand up and down his arm.

He moved, trying not to whip his limb out of her grasp, and leaned back in his chair, intertwining his fingers and resting them behind his head. "I don't know about that. It's more fun for me to be there."

Susie finished tying the next ribbon and said, "Did you play in high school or college?"

"High school," he said quickly. This was turning down a road he wasn't used to, but they may as well know now.

"Hockey's fun to watch. I went to a few games when I was in college." Becca gave him a half-smile, and he felt like his insides were ablaze.

Susie's head whipped back in his direction. "Where did you go to college, Colton?"

"I, uh, didn't go anywhere. I started working in construction my senior year of high school and found I loved it."

Becca looked up, a curious expression on her face before her focus turned back to the fabric in her hands. After a few minutes of silence, she spoke up, a determined expression causing Colton's attraction for her to grow in a leap.

"There's something about finding something you love and being able to support yourself with it." She grinned at him before looking back to the project in her lap.

He couldn't agree more. But along with that, he was beginning to realize that even though he loved his job, he was missing someone to love. Thinking over his occupation, he noted that by becoming a project manager, he'd have the freedom to stay in one place more often than as a finish carpenter. But he'd only get that job if he was able to secure the subdivision in Sage Creek.

He and Becca hadn't talked much about it over the past couple of days, and he wondered if her feelings toward the subdivision had changed at all. His heart was more open to the idea of love than it had been in probably his entire life, but he was falling for a girl who would be hurt by him getting his promotion.

He took a breath and blew out, trying to relax. Nothing was certain until the vote on Wednesday, so he might as well not let his mind get out of control just yet.

CHAPTER 15

Becca was surprised to hear Colton admit he coached little league hockey. Somehow it fit, and a part of her warmed to the idea, especially when she thought that he did it for fun, without a boy on the team. And then the fact that he already knew Tanner. Colton was surprising her around every turn.

"We should head to Grillo's for dinner," Susie suggested as they wrapped up for the night. She piled the decorations on the table and put her scissors back in the bag on the floor.

"What's Grillo's?" Colton asked, picking up several scraps of ribbon on the table and placing them in his palm.

Susie's face beamed. "It's this great restaurant and bar just down the highway. It'll be the perfect place to celebrate getting things back on track."

Becca watched Susie, who watched Colton, and then turned so the girl wouldn't see her smirk. It was obvious she was going for the builder, and even though a small tug of jealousy pulled at Becca's chest thinking about it, she knew it was better that than falling for the guy only to find out he liked someone else.

"I'm ready for a quiet night in," Becca said, putting her tools away.

"Becca, when is the last time you went out and had some fun? Just come tonight." Susie's voice was pleading, bordering on whining, and Becca thought about walking out the door right then.

"I'll go if Becca goes," Colton said with a mischievous grin.

Just short of getting on her knees, Susie thrust out her lips and full-on pouted, making her look like a fish.

Becca rolled her eyes. "Fine, but I'm not staying out all night. And can we go somewhere besides Grillo's?" She didn't need to relive all the memories of her time with Peter, not with how complicated her feelings were for Colton. She'd been avoiding that place for the last eighteen months.

Susie squealed with delight and threaded her arm through Becca's. "Oh, please. There isn't much else that's open, and it will be fun to get some dancing in." She did a little shimmy, and Becca almost backed out right there.

"Where is it? I don't think I've seen it here in town." Colton's voice caused Becca to turn in his direction.

"It's in between here and the next town over. Still in the county for our flower girl." Susie's voice held a little sarcasm, and Becca gritted her teeth, feeling her defenses rise.

They walked out of the rec center, and Susie looked up, pulling on the door to make sure it was secure. "My car is in the shop. Can we take one of yours?" she asked, leaning into Colton and looking up at him.

Becca frowned. Could the girl be any more obvious?

"I have my truck. It's down at the hotel." Colton shrugged his shoulder, which caused Susie to take a step back.

"Great. That'll be so fun. I haven't been in a truck in so long." Susie batted her eyes yet again.

Becca cringed, second-guessing her decision to come

tonight. If she was just going to be the third wheel, she'd be wishing she were at home the entire time.

They walked down Main Street to the hotel, with Susie jabbering on about everything that had happened in her life. Susie came from a family of money, but her parents had always been jet-setting to new places, leaving Susie in the care of one of the town residents. If anyone had been raised by the entire town, it was Susie Jones. From the sound of her stories, Becca almost felt bad for her, knowing her own short time away from the small town had been more adventurous than the girl's highlight reel.

Guilt flooded her just after the thought, knowing she shouldn't be happy for the experiences that resulted in her family's deaths.

"Becca, are you there?" Susie's hand passed over Becca's face several times before Becca pushed it away.

"What?"

"We were just talking about our favorite kind of music. What's yours?" Susie's eyebrows pinched together, focused on Becca's answer.

"I like anything but jazz. I just can't do it."

Colton chuckled. "I agree. One song is fine, but a whole bunch in a row? That's just too much." He motioned to his dark-green Chevy and pushed a button on his fob, making the lights flash and the truck beep.

Susie laughed. "You lock your truck here? In Sage Creek? We have a crime record of, like, negative one."

"This is a company vehicle, and I've been robbed before. Life's just easier when you've taken all the precautions necessary." He gave her a quick nod and turned to Becca. She gave him a small smile, sharing in the inside joke from when she'd told him about being robbed in college.

"Oh," was all Susie responded.

With only one row in the truck, Becca felt the irritation

grow as Susie slid over to the middle. As much as she wanted to stay neutral when it came to her feelings for Colton, it seemed her jealousy was rearing its head.

The drive to Grillo's didn't take long, but Becca was surprised at how clean the inside of Colton's truck was. She'd expected to be pushing around old drink cups and cupcake wrappers with her feet, but everything looked to be in order, not even a spot of dust on the dash. He hadn't had much to do since he got there, so maybe that was the reason?

Susie fiddled with the stations, allowing them to only hear about half of each song before she turned the knob to find another. That was the one downside to living near a canyon: the reception for normal stations wasn't as good. Not that Becca noticed since she rarely drove her car anymore.

When they pulled up to the restaurant, Becca knew she couldn't go inside. Too many memories were in there. Her first time meeting Peter just before she left for college, where they spent summer date nights, and where they hung out three days before their supposed wedding.

"Are you coming, Becca? The music sounds great." Susie started swaying her hips and moving her arms in the air, looking ridiculous from Becca's point of view.

"I'm coming." Maybe this would be good. Maybe she could finally get past Peter and the memories. Grillo's was the farthest she'd gone out of Sage Creek since the accident, but then again, it wasn't out of the county. Maybe she'd work her way up to leaving the canyon soon enough.

Baby steps, Becca.

The other two entered the dark restaurant, leaving Becca at the threshold. She took several breaths and finally found the courage to step forward.

As soon as her foot touched the floor, the sights and smells, the lights and music, all came crashing back at once.

She stumbled and was surprised to find strong arms holding her up.

"Are you okay? Let's get you to a table." Colton studied her face and then turned, keeping his arm around her waist to hold her up. The same tingling she'd felt every time he touched her erupted around his fingers, and she felt safe once again at his side.

When they found a table open, she sat back, breathing in through her nose and out through her mouth. She turned her head, spotting Susie near the bar, a playful look on her face as she talked to someone sitting there. Was she not really interested in Colton? The confusion caused her to close her eyes for several seconds, her brain back to focusing on the barrage of memories attacking her from her relationship with Peter.

Colton took the chair next to her, poised at the edge of it as if ready to defend her or rush to her aid if need be. "Can I get you a drink or some food?"

She opened her eyes, seeing him only inches away from her face. The softness of his expression gave her the urge to lean forward and kiss him. As she focused on his face, the nightmares seemed to fade away into the background.

"I think I just need some food." She pulled the menus from behind the ketchup and mustard, handing him one. She already knew what she was getting without glancing at it, but it was something to distract her from staring at him. And it kept her from talking about her little dizzy spell.

Colton looked up to ask, "What's good here?"

Biting her bottom lip, Becca glanced over the menu with fresh eyes. She'd never had to recommend anything here before, and she wracked her brain for favorites of her friends.

"They have some great loaded fries, and their chips and salsa are really good. As for real food, they make one of the best burgers I've ever had. Cheese, bacon, avocado…all the good stuff." Well, that good stuff meant her figure was curvier than most, but she was okay with that.

He pursed his lips and nodded, looking down at the menu again. "I think you sold me on the burger, minus the avocado, though."

Putting a hand to her chest, Becca took an exaggerated gasp. "No avocado? How can you live without the creamy deliciousness of the avocado?"

"The texture is all wrong. I just can't do it, Cap'n." His fake accent had her giggling, and then his smile after made her insides flip. He finally said, "Do they have good non-loaded fries?" His eyes locked onto hers, and the tension between them was almost palpable.

He licked his lips quickly, drawing her attention to them. They appeared soft, and when she raised her gaze to his eyes, he seemed to be studying her features just like she was his.

"What can I get y'all?" a high-pitched voice asked behind them. Colton broke his gaze first, giving the waitress his order. Becca gave hers, hardly turning from Colton. How had her feelings changed so quickly when she'd only known him a handful of days? She was falling for him, and no matter what she did, she would probably end up with heartbreak.

But was it worth it? She'd had more fun with him around than she had in the past few years. Maybe not every risk turned out how she wanted it to, but she was young. And as it went, she'd been living like one of the retirees in town rather than the twenty-seven-year-old she was.

Colton turned to Becca. "Looks like she found someone to flirt with already," he said, pointing in Susie's direction.

Becca leaned to the side and saw Susie talking to the same man next to the bar. "And here I was thinking she was going after you." The moment the words popped out, Becca wished she could rein them back in, feeling the heat rise to her cheeks.

Colton shook his head, his eyebrows raised in disbelief. "She's the kind of girl who doesn't know what she wants."

Leaning forward, Becca pursed her lips, curious as to what he meant. "How would you know that?"

"I've spent my life reading people, and for the most part, I can get most of the details correct."

"And what have you figured out about Susie?" Becca glanced between the girl across the room and the man sitting next to her, her interest peaked.

Colton shifted back in his seat, resting an arm on the table mere inches from Becca's hand. "She was an only child, but her parents weren't around much. So she seeks attention from anyone who'll give it to her. She looks completely put together, but that's to hide the insecurities she's feeling."

"Wow, what you just said was scary accurate." Becca looked at him, her mouth open a bit in surprise. She searched his face but found no arrogance from her admission. Taking a breath, she said, "I'm a little worried to ask, but what can you tell about me?"

Her question must have caused some discomfort because he leaned forward, his arms resting on his knees and his hands studying his fingernails. "Um, well, I did say for the most part. I have to say that you're still a bit of a mystery to me, Becca Taylor."

Becca reached out and grabbed his upper arm, turning him toward her. "That's it? I'm a mystery?" she said, unable to keep the sarcasm out of her words. Was he just telling her that so he wouldn't upset her? Or was she really that hard to read?

"I've gotten a few different vibes from you since I've been here, and for the most part, I can tell you've been through a lot, that you're trying to figure out what you want out of life."

Becca's mouth opened, and she wished she could process what to say. She closed it as she let the words pass through her mind again. As much as some of it hurt, he was right. She'd been on autopilot for so long, just trying to make it through each day, that she'd forgotten to look forward to things, to be the adventurous girl she'd once been.

Colton moved his hand over to rest on top of Becca's on the table. "I didn't want to offend you..." His words trailed off as if he was having just as hard of a time of coming up with something to say.

Glancing at their hands together, Becca wondered if this was all some dream she'd wake up from in a few minutes. But as the seconds ticked by, she turned her gaze back to him.

"No, I think I needed to hear that." She paused a moment, deciding to take that one little risk and get to know him more.

"So, Colton Maxfield, what do you think about Sage Creek? Too small for you?"

He shook his head. "No, it reminds me of home at times. The slower pace is something I missed when I first got to Denver, and now I realize how nice it is to not have a jam-packed schedule."

Becca blinked, as if that would help her process every-thing he'd been saying. "But if you got the contract, you'd be pretty busy, I'd imagine. Especially if your boss is how you describe him. He'll probably want a job that usually takes a year to be done in four months."

Colton nodded. "I hadn't thought about it like that. But it would be more time to hang around and get to know more people in Sage Creek." The intensity of his gaze caused Becca to shift in her seat, focusing on her nails instead of his face.

"So, you told me your mother still lives where you grew up for the most part. If you moved back to a small town, would she follow you?" Becca hadn't clearly thought through the question before it escaped her lips. She glanced up, seeing something like hope there, and realized she'd made it sound as though she wanted him to stick around for a while.

"I had a friend once ask why I didn't just find another construction company near her. Dream Homes has been really good to me, training me when I knew next to nothing. As much as I miss seeing my mom, I'm grateful for the work and the environment. I love creating a place where people can make memories."

"I totally understand that," Becca said, nodding. "I love flowers and creating a type of art with them. There's just something about putting all of yourself into it. A simple arrangement can make a pretty visual with how I arrange them."

"You definitely have a knack for that. I wouldn't even know the first thing about how to arrange flowers."

Becca smiled. "I'm not sure I really do either. It's more of an ingrained thing, and I just move things around as I go. I wish I could see the big picture beforehand, but I guess that's what keeps people coming back in a small town."

"Have you ever wanted to live anywhere else?" He took a sip of water, his eyes studying her so intensely that she had to look away.

Flattening out the paper from the straw, she said, "I did. I went to college. I thought about moving away when I was engaged, but that didn't quite work out." She noted the surprise on his face and chuckled.

"I didn't realize you were engaged. What happened?" Colton's eyes were wide like it was the first time he'd learned of it. In a town as small as Sage Creek, it was next to impossible for people to keep secrets, especially ones as big as a failed wedding from a stranger. Becca was surprised he hadn't heard yet.

The waitress walked up with their food, pausing the conversation a moment as things got settled.

"That's a first. I can't believe the whole town didn't blab about it at the first mention of me." Fresh pain seared through her chest. The embarrassment of the whole thing caused her cheeks to burn, and she was grateful for the low light to camouflage some of it.

When Colton didn't say anything, she sighed. "He didn't want to be with me in the end. Honestly, I don't really know what happened. I think that's the hardest part about the whole thing. I got up on my wedding day—hair done, nails done, wedding dress on—and Mrs. Watkins had to come in and tell me he'd left town without even a note." She gave him a fake smile, doing all she could to hold back the wall of tears. "My best friend, Danielle, found out he'd been dating someone from his company at the same time and had decided he'd rather have a city girl than one who was stuck in a small town."

Motioning around the room, Colton asked, "Does this place have any ties to your ex-fiancé?"

Becca could only nod. She leaned forward and took a bite of the burger. Colton did the same, and she watched as the satisfaction on his face was well worth it.

"You weren't kidding. What's the secret?" he asked, pointing to the burger in his hand.

With a quick shrug, she said, "I don't know. All I know is I like it."

She took another bite and watched as Susie walked out on the dance floor with the guy she'd been talking to. Becca had forgotten about the dancing, and she just hoped Susie wouldn't force her to dance with some random guy there. Even with Colton, she wasn't sure she'd survive the dance. Not that it was the worst thing in the world, but with Becca's two left feet, it made it hard to leave the dance floor with anyone not limping.

"Are there many young people in Sage Creek?" Colton asked.

Becca laughed. "Are you talking about married young people or single young people?"

Colton grinned and looked around as if trying to decide. "Single young people?"

Shaking her head, Becca said, "Not many. It's definitely not the best dating pool, but I haven't been worried about that for a while." Her heart felt betrayed at the words, but Colton didn't flinch.

"How long has it been since your ex left?"

Why did he keep bringing him up? "One year, six months, and three days. He'd been with me through a lot, and I thought we'd be together forever."

A flash of a smile appeared as she gave him the count, and then he frowned as though someone had taken away his favorite toy.

"I take it you're still hung up on him, then?" Colton looked at her through hooded eyes, probably worried he'd scare her off.

Becca dabbed a napkin along her chin, buying time to phrase the right words. "No, I'm just weird like that. I know the exact amount of time that's passed from significant things in my past. My parents and brother died five years, six months, and thirteen days ago."

Colton's Adam's apple bobbed a few times, a slight pity in his eyes.

They ate in silence, watching the other people move and dance around the room. When Colton finished, he wiped his hands on a napkin and held out his hand. "May I have this dance, Miss Taylor?"

Becca froze. What was she supposed to do or say? "Um,

would you like both feet to be functioning tomorrow?" Not her best line ever, but she had to at least warn him.

"I'm willing to take that risk." He smiled, his eyes locked onto hers, and she was glad she was sitting down. Those baby browns were doing a number on her nervous system.

She stared at his hand for a few more seconds before putting hers in it, letting him pull her up. His fingers were rough with calluses, but his hand was warm, and hers seemed to fit perfectly inside it. The song changed right before they got to their spot on the dance floor, a slower tempo.

He took her hand in his and placed his other on her hip. She was used to wrapping both arms around the guy's neck, so this was different for her, but she put her hand on his shoulder and moved with his guidance. The steps weren't big or flashy, but she didn't step on him at all.

She took in a deep breath, enjoying his woodsy cologne. It reminded her of her father, and she closed her eyes as they kept swaying to the music. By the end of the song, she opened her eyes to see she was laying her head on his chest.

Taking a step back, she said, "I'm so sorry. But thank you for making this the first dance where people walk away unharmed."

Feeling flustered, she turned and took long strides until she made it back to the table. Her skin was on fire where he'd touched her, and she now felt the loss of the heat from his body.

Why were her emotions going berserk? She hadn't felt like this even with Peter, the shocks and jolts of electricity, and she couldn't figure out what made Colton so different. Something she'd have to think about later in the safety of her own home.

CHAPTER 16

Watching Becca walk off the dance floor, Colton felt like a part of him was walking away. He waited a few seconds and then walked back over, hoping not to scare her too much. She'd been through a lot. He'd been so young when his father never returned, but he couldn't imagine losing his entire family all in one day. And then to have her fiancé just leave without telling her why? That was a lot to overcome.

He was somewhat surprised the chatty people of the town hadn't let it slip that she'd almost been married, but then again, she was beautiful and amazing. Why wouldn't she have dated or had a long-term relationship before he'd waltzed into town a few days before?

The attraction between them had been almost crackling as they'd talked, and more than ever, he hoped he could figure something out, some way to have a real relationship with the girl he was beginning to love.

He moved his chair next to her so he was facing the dance floor instead of her, hoping to keep the atmosphere comfortable. He wanted to say something but wasn't sure what the appropriate response would be. *Thanks for dancing with me. You smell amazing. I kind of like you.*

He shook his head, knowing he couldn't say that last part for sure. With how skittish she'd been with everything else, he didn't want to chase away what little footing he'd made too soon.

"Sorry I'm so awkward." Her words were shaky, and she grimaced.

Against what his mind kept shouting, he reached over and took her hand in his, rubbing his thumb over the back of her hand.

"You're good. Life is awkward for the most part, so I wouldn't worry about this. In fact, I think our dance was pretty much perfect."

She turned to look at him, but he couldn't meet her eyes without the attraction growing within him. She'd see it, too, and then she'd run, just like she'd run the day of the tour. Or just now after their dance.

Susie came over, laughing and giggling. "Are you guys having fun?"

Colton nodded, and even though Becca was a little more hesitant, at least she was smiling.

"Great. If you don't mind, I'm going to stay a little longer and hang out with Todd here. He'll give me a ride back home if you two want to leave." She waved at them as Todd pulled her back onto the dance floor, dancing and laughing.

Colton had always envied people who were that carefree, mostly because he wanted to be like them. But there had always been a lot of responsibilities in his life. As fun as it looked, he was just fine sitting on the side, watching. He turned to Becca and said, "I'm ready whenever you are. It's been a long day."

He caught her yawning, which triggered his own yawning, leaving both of them laughing afterward.

"I think it's time we head back." Colton stood and moved his seat out of the way so she could get by, and they walked out of the restaurant and over to his truck. He took a couple strides faster so he could open the door for her, and she gave him a look he couldn't quite read.

Once he made it around to his door, he slid in and started the truck, reveling in the sound of the engine.

"You kind of like this truck, don't you?" Becca said with a laugh.

"Maybe." He grinned at her. "There are a lot of upgrades from my old truck, and I just like that this one starts up every time I try."

She nodded. "I can understand that. I've had my old Civic since I could drive. My parents bought her off of one of the people in town just a few streets over from my house. There are days when she's a little more temperamental than I would like, but she's got a lot of good memories."

"My old truck just sits in the driveway now. I drive this just about everywhere, but I just couldn't part with the other one. Like you said, a lot of my life was spent in that truck, driving from worksite to worksite or from Denver up to Boulder to visit. There's something about those memories you just can't give up."

Turning onto the main highway, Colton sped up, flipping on his brights for the small distance.

Becca turned toward him. "You said you started working in construction out of high school. Have you ever wanted to do anything else?"

Colton's breath hitched, and he took a minute before answering. "I wanted to be a pilot when I was younger, thinking it would keep a piece of my dad with me. But then I realized making some money to help my mom pay the bills was better than taking out a loan to get all the training I needed for it. I haven't really looked back since." He paused, adjusting his grip on the steering wheel. "What about you? Did you want to be something other than a flower girl?"

Becca laughed, the wide smile brightening her features even with the dim light. "I got a degree in interior design, and when I was with Peter, I thought it was perfect. Builder, designer. I thought we could one day start up our own company together. That only lasted a few months after I realized that working for Peter would have ended our relationship. His idea of how things should look was much different than mine. So I started up the flower shop and have been working on jewelry since. I've thought about starting a website to sell it since just about every woman in town owns at least three pieces I've made."

The cab went silent, and Colton glanced over to see Becca's hands twisting together, the lights of the dash reflecting off her eyes.

She cleared her throat. "Do you ever wonder what your life would have been like had your father not left?"

Colton bit the inside of his cheek, debating whether or not to tell her. "Every once in a while I do. After football season my senior year, I had to find a way to help out because my mom wasn't able to work anymore. I had a scholarship for football and knew, even with government assistance, that she wouldn't make it four years without something to help. I gave up the scholarship to keep working for Dream Homes—well, Summers Construction back then. So sometimes I wonder what it would've been like to play college football." He glanced over at her, hoping she wouldn't think he was trying to toot his own horn.

He was surprised by the touch of her hand on his arm and the concern on her face. "I'm so sorry. As someone who's lost her parents, I know that doesn't help much, but I can sympathize somewhat."

Turning to her, he gave her a quick nod and a thin-lipped smile. "Thank you. That means a lot."

They drove in silence for a few moments, and he finally said, "Like I said, memories. Sometimes they're good ones, and others I like to remember because they've helped me grow."

Becca wiped away a tear and turned to him. "I really like that. Not looking at memories as bad, but looking at them for what they changed about you."

He smiled, excited that she'd admitted she liked something he'd said. Soon enough came the turn off for Sage Creek.

As he drove down the street, he said, "Am I taking you home?"

"Uh, yeah. I'm definitely not a night owl anymore."

"Me either. Those days are behind me, I think."

Pulling into her driveway, the headlights shone over the garage and porch. It was the type of home his mother had always wanted, and Colton still hoped he could fulfill that dream for her before she died. But this house, with the corbels near the peaks and the soft gray color was perfect for Becca, matching her personality better than he'd seen any house match someone.

As she moved to get out of the truck, he said, "I'm glad you came with us. It would've been awkward with— I mean, I'm glad we could get to know a little more about each other." He rolled his lips in, wishing he could reach out and pull the words back in. He just didn't want things to get weird.

She paused and turned to him. "I'm glad I did too. Thank you for everything." After staring at him a moment longer, she nodded and slid out. She shut the door before running to the side of her house and disappearing.

As Colton backed out, he wasn't quite sure what he'd done to help her, but he was glad he'd been there.

CHAPTER 17

On Sunday, Becca met up with a few of the council members at the land for the subdivision, and she found that the arguments she'd formulated in her head weren't as effective as she'd originally thought. But as she caught sight of Colton loading something into the back of a truck for one of the families near the fountain, she realized the fight she'd held onto for so long about the subdivision was fading.

Maybe it wouldn't be awful to have a few more new faces around. And the handsome stranger made her secretly hope the subdivision would go through so he'd be able to stay a little longer and they'd be able to figure out if they would be good together or not.

But since they'd known each other less than a week, she'd just have to keep those thoughts under wraps.

That afternoon and into the next day, it rained, pouring buckets and buckets of water around Sage Creek. Becca liked the rain when she didn't have to leave her house, but getting wet and cold wasn't her favorite thing to do. She opened the shop a few hours late on Monday and ended up closing early when not many people came by. Most of the town seemed to have the same idea, folding up into their own houses.

She hadn't been by the rec center to see how the decorations were turning out, but she hoped Susie would be fine without her help. Or that she'd ask again if she really did need it.

Locking the door of the flower shop, she pulled out her umbrella, tucking the rain jacket around her for warmth against the cold droplets. She took a couple of steps into the road, and her rain boots sank into what looked like mud. Looking up the street, she saw mud everywhere.

Her stomach tensed and she froze, panic taking over. Becca wasn't sure what to do. The town hadn't had a major flood in over forty years, but with the amount of rain falling, she knew it was inevitable.

Changing directions, she moved up to Town Hall where the mud was even thicker and wetter. Several people came out of houses, saying their basements were flooding. They gathered in a group, umbrellas shielding the small group as several of them began chatting to each other.

Running up to Tara Jones's house, she asked, "What can I do to help?"

"We need sandbags or something. It's all coming in through the windows." The woman was only a few years older than Becca, but her composure at a moment like this was something Becca admired.

The mayor walked out of Town Hall joining the group just down from the fountain. "We've got plenty of supplies for making sandbags over by the recreation building. We can split into two groups, one for making the bags and the other for diverting the water away from homes

"Give me a shovel, and I can start working on that." The mayor held out his key ring and Becca accepted it with a nod.

She plodded through the mud and water down the block

to open the shed, a couple of the townspeople following her. A slew of shovels, rakes, and other tools had been shoved into the corner, and she pulled out a few, hoping to recruit people along the way.

She carried three shovels and walked as fast as she could, moving back toward Town Hall. From there, she followed the water trails, moving up through the thick pines. The water got faster and faster, making it difficult to move up the trail. Even with all the pine trees blocking some of the landslide, there was so much water that they couldn't hold it all back.

"Where you going?" a deep voice said behind her.

Becca turned her head and said, "I'm going to see what I can do about the water. People's homes are flooding, and if we can divert the water somehow, we might be able to save the other buildings nearby."

Droplets were streaming down Colton's face, and his hair was plastered to his head. He walked right next to her, reaching out to take two of the shovels.

Arriving at the crest of the hill, she found the trail surrounding the pond was completely covered in water. She moved to investigate and found that the water was starting to creep up to her knees.

"Don't go any farther," Colton warned, grabbing her arm. "The floodwater might pull you under." He led her back from the rushing water.

Releasing her arm once she was safe, he turned to look at the damage, rubbing his arms against the cold. "There's a bunch of water coming down the mountain. That's filling up the pond, which is flooding the town."

"Okay, so what do we do?"

"We're going to have to dig some trenches or build a blockade to cause the water to change course. The only problem is, it's filling up so fast in the pond that it will make it hard to make any changes down here below."

"Is there a way to fix it up higher?"

He frowned but nodded. "Yeah, but it's not the best idea in my opinion. The water is much faster than what's emptying out from the pond."

"Do we go down and sandbag, then?" Becca searched the landscape, hoping a solution would pop into her head.

"I think if we get the sandbags up here, we'll have a better chance of saving the buildings below from a lot of flooding, maybe even all the water."

He turned and walked down the trail back to the city building, Becca almost skipping to keep up with his long strides. Several more people milled about now, and as Colton passed them, he motioned them all to follow him. Becca couldn't help but smile as the confidence he exuded helped lead the people over to the shed where Becca had found the tools.

"Okay, we've got to work together and fast. I need four volunteers to fill sandbags from that large pile of sand we have just around the corner of the shed." He nodded as four people stepped forward, and he gave out the shovels in his hand.

After opening the shed, he spoke again. "We have two wheelbarrows which we'll use to drive the sandbags to the bottom of the trail, and then we'll use a human chain to get the sandbags up to the top and in place. If you know of anyone else who can help out, go grab them and come right back. We have several houses already getting water, and we want to prevent as much damage as possible."

There was a slight pause after he finished speaking, as if the crowd was waiting for more instructions. And then they broke apart, several of them running to other homes and buildings, directing people to the trail as they went.

"Where do you want me?" Becca asked Colton, surprised that the person the town was turning to was the stranger. But it felt more right than anything.

One side of his mouth quirked up, and he said, "You can either join the line up the hill or come with me to set the sandbags around the pond." The tone of his voice sounded hopeful toward the end, and she nodded.

"I can help set them."

She waited as Colton made sure the people filling sandbags had everything they needed and then grabbed two extra shovels, taking them once again to the trail.

They'd almost made it to the top of the hill when Becca slipped in the mud, falling forward. Colton ended up sliding next to her as he tried to get a grip on the trail.

"What a mess!" Becca said, standing up and shaking off the chunks of mud that had stuck to her hand.

Colton reached for her, and together they leaned against the pine trees, finally making it to the flat path on top. He took his shovel and started hitting it against a branch near them.

"What are you doing?" Becca asked, a bit horrified that he would be destroying one of the beautiful trees around the pond.

"That's a big patch of mud, and if we don't have some kind of traction for the people holding on to the sandbags, we won't be able to even get them up here. I thought I'd try a few branches and see if that will make it less slippery."

Where was this guy from? The fact that he could think of solutions with the little they had up there was something Becca admired. And it showed how much he'd come to care about the town, which was something Peter had never done before.

She raised her shovel and did the best she could, hitting

the tip of it into the side of a low-hanging branch. It was going to be a long day, but it was worth it to save their little town.

CHAPTER 18

Becca was grateful when the rain stopped. The mud had slowed and then stopped after they'd been able to block the water from the pond and divert any runoff, keeping the damage lower than it could have been. They'd been working for the past eighteen hours, filling sandbags and digging trenches, all in the hopes of saving their town.

What Becca loved the most was that everyone was there, pitching in, helping one another with this or that. It was how a small town should be, and she hoped it would stay that way forever.

But as they worked, she realized the disparity in ages. Folks with white hair outnumbered the ones without, and the younger kids were fewer than she'd remembered. In the early twenties to the mid-forties range, there were only about fifty or sixty of them, and as the older people tired quickly, the younger ones had to keep working through the long night hours.

It seemed as though everything Colton had said at that opening meeting, she was now just realizing. Taking a sip from a water bottle someone handed her, she sat up against a building, still feeling the chill and exhaustion down to her bones. She hadn't worked like this in a long time, but as long as she could help stave off the damage to others' homes, she'd do it again and again.

As many people were slowing down for the evening, Becca had an idea and hurried back to her house. Going into the nursery out back, she trimmed several different flowers and brought them back to the worktable in the flower shop. Pulling out paper, she started wrapping them in small bouquets and layering the bundles into a basket. She walked out and started looking for people on the street, handing them to anyone she saw.

"These are beautiful, Becca," Jenny Hinckley said, smelling the bouquet. "What do I owe you?"

Becca raised a hand and shook her head. "No charge. I just hope it's a bright spot in this long day."

She left the woman with a smile and moved on to the next house. House after house, she was happy to see the smiles and a little bit of relief at the thought that their houses weren't going to be damaged even more. Tara Jones handed her umbrella to her as she came to her house, thanking her for the quick work she'd done to help solve the problem.

Out of flowers, she moved past Town Hall and up the hill to the pond, curious as to what it looked like now after all of the water. Several men walked past her on their way back to town, and she smiled at them all before continuing on. When she got to the top, she saw Colton was the only one left.

She stood behind the trees, trying to decide if she should just turn around and head back to town or stay and say something to him. He'd been nothing but sweet the past few days, and she was beginning to think he wasn't anywhere near the person Peter had become.

Taking a step forward, she smiled. "All the other ones left. You're still here?" she asked, curious.

Colton turned and smiled at her, and she had to move forward to keep her legs from buckling at the sight. "Almost done. Just got this last couple of boards to put in, and then we should be good."

"What is it you've done here?" She stepped next to him, trying not to stare at his eyes. They seemed to keep her mesmerized, and the fact that he wasn't there to stay caused her to pause. She'd admired the work ethic he'd shown over these past two days, and it seemed he was turning into the knight in shining armor she'd always pictured as a young girl. But once he went back to Denver, she couldn't go with him. In fact, the thought of crossing the border of the county turned her insides into a knitted cloth.

"We worked to build up the bank and then put this little wall up." He stepped to the side and waved his arm around, acting like a model on one of those reality game shows. She had gone down to help with the cleanup of some of the nearby houses after they'd placed enough sandbags the day before and hadn't come back up until now.

Becca walked up to it, glancing over at the pond below. It had gone down several inches in the past day. "This doesn't look like a little wall. Is it kind of like a dam?"

Colton nodded. "Just to help the town in case it ever rains like that again. When the water starts to fill in the pocket below, it raises up the wall, and then the pressure from the water causes the wall to stay up, holding back the flood. I remembered hearing about it at a convention my boss sent me to last year, and I convinced the people this would be the best thing for the future."

"You didn't ask me." She felt a little hurt that he hadn't at least included her in the project. But that was ridiculous. It wasn't like she was in charge of the town or anything, but he'd seemed concerned about her opinion on other things.

"We decided when we were cleaning things up. Are you okay with it?" He looked worried, and he reached his hand out and touched her upper arm, sending tingles sizzling through her body.

She shrugged. "As long as it helps out the town, I guess that's a good thing, right?" A sudden bout of worry shot through her. "Why are you helping us out? You don't even live here."

"Does that matter? When people are in need and I can do something to help, isn't that what I'm supposed to do?" He stared at her, the seriousness of his expression drawing her in, causing her to focus on his lips.

Her heart thumped out a few beats, and she was curious as to what his lips would feel like on hers. She shook her head a bit to clear the thoughts and then said, "Yes, I guess you're right."

He turned and looked at her basket with her umbrella in it. "Are you Red Riding Hood, going to visit her grandmother?"

With his loud chuckle, Becca rolled her eyes, enjoying the teasing expression on his face. "No, I just figured I'd deliver some bouquets of flowers to help some of the people have a good night."

"That's a good idea. I'm sure after all of the worry, your flowers brought them some joy."

Their eyes locked, and a tumultuous sea roared to life inside her, leaving her not knowing which way or what she was feeling.

She pointed to the dam. "Well, this will definitely give people in town some peace of mind."

The sun had gone down at that point, and the sky was quickly darkening.

"Did you come up here for some reason?" Colton asked.

"No, I wanted to see how things were, and I like to look at the pond sometimes. It helps calm me down, just like the fountain. It was one of my mother's favorite places to go."

Colton's hand reached for hers, warm against her cold fingers. "You miss them a lot, don't you?"

Becca nodded, a tear falling without her permission. "More than I care to admit. My brother was a lot of fun to hang out with, and sometimes I can still hear all their voices in my house. Not in a creepy way, just memories."

"I can understand that. At least you knew they loved you, though." His smile was sad, and she knew he was thinking about his father.

"They did that for sure. I remember inviting them over for a weekend to my apartment in Salt Lake. We laughed and played games until much later than we should've. But it's still the best last memory I have of them." She paused and then said, "Are you heading back to town?"

He gave a quick nod. "I'll be down in a minute. I just want to soak up the last bits of this."

"Are you leaving town?" Becca blurted, panic filling her chest.

He shook his head. "No, but it's so peaceful right here, and it's about the perfect temperature." He stepped over to one of the benches that had resurfaced from the receding water and sat down, tipping his head back to look at the sky.

Becca turned to look back at the trail to town and then glanced over at Colton, trying to decide what to do. She finally sat next to him, keeping some space in between. It was quiet for several moments, until the cold air seeped through the thin jacket she was wearing and she shivered.

"Do you want my jacket?" Colton said leaning forward and unzipping the jacket he wore.

Becca held out her hand. "No, I'll be all right."

"She says with teeth chattering." Colton grinned. "Not on my watch."

He slid over and wrapped the jacket around her shoulders, not moving away after. The instant warmth from the jacket helped her body warm up, but her teeth-chattering took a few more minutes to calm down.

Colton wrapped his arm around her and pulled her next to him, adding another heat source to her chill body. She couldn't help but smell his cologne on the jacket, and she took in little breaths, hoping he wouldn't see her enjoying it. That was the last thing she needed right now.

"I can see why you'd want to come back here, after college, I mean. This place is beautiful."

Tingles shot up her back and through her arms, not the effect from the cold. Peter had never said anything like that, and Becca just hoped Colton wasn't lying about it.

"Yes, it's beautiful. And the small-town community makes you feel like you're home. I was only in the city for a while, and while I enjoyed it, I never really got that settled feeling like I could live there forever. The minute I came back home, I knew this was where I had to be."

Colton nodded. "Did your fiancé want to stay here?"

Playing with the zipper on his jacket, Becca said, "He always claimed he did, but I don't think it was the truth. He'd grown up a few towns over, and I think once he saw what the city was like, he couldn't go back to the small-town life."

"Look!" Colton said, and Becca raised her eyes to where his finger was pointing. A shooting star crossed the sky, and she couldn't help but smile.

"I haven't seen one of those in a long time." She looked up at him and found he was staring at her.

"Me neither."

With only a brief hesitation, he leaned forward, his lips touching hers. The kiss was light at first, feathery and gentle, chasing away any lingering cold in her body. He slowly pulled back enough to look into her eyes, gauging her reaction.

Missing the warmth of his lips on hers, Becca moved forward and pressed her lips to his with more force, reaching her hand behind his neck and bring him even closer. The energy flowing between them was stronger than anything she'd felt before, her chest feeling as if fireworks had been lit inside.

When he pulled away, he smiled at her, and heat rushed to her cheeks. "I should probably get you home. We don't want to be out too late. You never know what will happen at this pond." He winked at her, and she wasn't quite sure what he meant by that comment. She wanted him to kiss her again, but she knew he was probably right.

They walked down the path, not saying anything. Becca was sure he could hear her heart pounding in her chest. A ways down the trail, he captured her hand, intertwining his fingers with hers. Electricity shot up her arm, and she turned and grinned at him.

Never did she think she would feel like this for a builder again, but here she was, underneath the stars, walking back into the town that held her heart.

She just hoped Colton wouldn't break it.

CHAPTER 19

By the time they made it out of the woods, Colton wondered why he'd never felt like this before. He'd surprised himself by leaning in and kissing Becca, but it had been a kiss like he'd never had before. Her lips were so soft, and she'd never thrown herself at him like most of the girls he'd known.

He didn't want to break the feeling with words, so they made it back to her house before he said anything.

"I hope you're all right." He looked into her eyes, hoping she didn't feel ashamed for the kiss.

She leaned up on her tiptoes and touched her lips to his again. Pulling back, she smiled. "I'm more than all right. Thank you for tonight." She stepped away and walked inside, waving to him before she shut the door completely.

He turned around, ready to jump off the stairs, when he saw someone staring through the window across the street. He wasn't sure what Becca felt about the neighbors knowing they'd kissed, so he walked casually down to the corner and fist-pumped the minute the street was empty.

He wasn't sure when he'd known it, but he really liked

this girl, and he hoped her reciprocation of the kiss meant she had feelings for him too. It had been so long since he'd dated anyone, really dated anyone, that he wasn't sure what happened next. And the fact that he wasn't some high-powered CEO and she still wanted to hang out with him was something. He would just have to figure it out as he went along, hoping he wouldn't screw up.

He couldn't help but wonder about the future. Becca was pretty set on staying in Sage Creek, and he was starting to love the place as well. If the subdivision went through, he'd have plenty of work for the next couple of years, but what would happen after that? Would he be able to make a life here in this small town?

Moving in the direction of his hotel, he was ready for a hot shower and some time to remember that kiss.

* * *

THE NEXT DAY, he didn't see Becca until late, as he'd gone to help clean out some of the basements that had been flooded. The people were generous and oftentimes brought him lunch or dinner or drinks, and he was very grateful for it. The hard work helped him pass the time, knowing that he'd see Becca at the council meeting that night. They hadn't had a chance to talk about her opinion on the land, and he hoped it had changed from all the information he'd shared with her.

After a quick shower and change, he hurried back to the center of town, tucking in a button-up shirt before walking into the building.

"You clean up nice," he heard someone say. Turning, disappointment washed over him as he saw it was Susie.

"Thank you. Are you on the town council?"

She shook her head. "No, I just thought it would be fun to sit in on it tonight."

Colton nodded, wondering what could make someone sit through a boring meeting like this on a weeknight.

He moved in the direction of the council room, and when he walked in, his eyes met Becca's. He couldn't help but grin like a little schoolboy.

She smiled back and tucked a piece of hair behind her ear, the rest of it cascading over the table. She turned to look down at her papers, a red flush creeping into her cheeks. He hoped it was the result of thinking about their kiss because it had been hard for him to get the memory out of his head all day.

The meeting commenced shortly after, and the subdivision was first on the docket. "Has everyone had time to study the subdivision proposal?" Mayor Watkins asked.

All the heads at the table nodded, and he continued. "Are we ready to put it to a vote?"

The guy that was so angry the week before spoke up, and Colton had to do everything he could to not roll his eyes. "With the amount of rain we sustained this last week, I'm worried that adding extra houses will make the ground less stable for the town."

Standing up, Colton raised an arm and said, "Less stable? The subdivision is all the way at the other end of town. There's no way—"

"Please sit down, Mr. Maxfield. This is the time for the council to discuss." The mayor winked at him and smiled, trying to reassure him it would be okay.

"I don't want to give my consent without having all the proper tests conducted. I would like to hire people to study the soil and the water, making sure that any extra houses will be sustained," the angry man continued.

Extra tests? That could take months, and with the summer starting, Colton knew his boss wanted to get started on the project as soon as possible. They could usually get the house sold by the time the house was framed, and it was difficult to do much work in the snow.

Raising a hand, Colton started again, "Mayor, Town Council, I urge you to make a decision soon. There are a lot of people who've been looking at the plans and have shown interest in these properties. These people can help make a difference in this community and keep it from dying. They can help to dig out the houses when it floods and contribute to the overall economy. But we prefer not to start working on things when it's wintertime."

With more firmness this time, the mayor used a hand to signal for Colton to sit down. "We will take this into consideration, Colton. Now, I must ask you again to keep silent, or you'll be asked to leave the room."

Sitting back with his arms folded against his chest, Colton blew out a breath. He needed to focus. This was why he was in this town. It was his livelihood, and without it, there wouldn't really be a future with Becca anyway.

After several more minutes of discussion, the council voted for the requested tests to be conducted and that a final decision be made within the next two weeks. It wasn't the best answer Colton could have hoped for, but a matter of days was a lot better than three months down the road. The man who'd been debating didn't look pleased with such a quick turnaround, but it was a good compromise for both sides. Plus, that meant Colton would be in town for the Founder's Day Festival.

Pulling out his phone, Colton texted his boss the news.

Two weeks? That'll be the final answer, though, right? Adam replied.

That's what the mayor said. If we have everything ready to go, we shouldn't be too far behind.

It took a few more minutes before his boss answered again.

I'm counting on this. Make it happen, Colton. You'll get a bonus once this goes through.

He'd never been one to worry about getting a bonus, but with the future he pictured in his head, he'd have to put down roots in Sage Creek, and every little bit he'd saved over the years that hadn't gone to his mother would hopefully go toward that future.

Toward the end of the meeting, Becca had a thought. The council had talked about the weather and where things could be allotted to build up the town again. As per usual, the budget didn't stretch as far as she wanted it to, making her brain work overtime.

She hadn't said much at the meeting, knowing there had been enough protesting against the subdivision, and she found that part of her wanted the subdivision to go forward now as it would be a way for her to see Colton more. But that was selfish. Would the new homes be for the best in their small town?

But what about the realization that the town needed young blood to help pump life back into it? Colton's ready smile and chocolate-brown eyes distracted her from across the room, reminding her of all the work he'd put into helping the town.

"Is there anything else we need to discuss? Becca, what did we miss on the agenda?" the mayor asked, bringing her back to the present.

"In regards to the flooding, I thought it might be a good

idea to hold an old-time bake-off or raffle that would raise funds to help those with property damage. We could hold it at the Founder's Day Festival, and it would be something the community could come together on."

There was silence for several seconds, and Becca wanted to squirm, wishing she could take back the suggestion.

The mayor finally said, "I like that idea. I think it'll be a great support of the community and can help our town get right back to where we were. Would you mind organizing that? Getting the word out and letting Susie know to include it in her program?"

Becca nodded, the excitement of adding a new project rushing through her. The meeting ended, and she gathered up her things, distracted as she tried to figure out exactly what they should do for the fundraiser.

She could feel Colton's eyes on her, and he moved out of his seat to just behind her, leaning forward and whispering, "I'd like to raffle something."

Once they got into the hallway, she said, "You want to raffle something? Can I ask what it is?"

With a mischievous smile, Colton said, "You'll just have to see."

She didn't like that thought, especially if she was putting together the event. "What if I threaten to auction you off as a date?" Her eyes widened, surprised she'd said it. Although there were several ladies in town who would probably bid for him, she wasn't sure she wanted to compete with them.

He leaned his hand against the wall, crossing one leg over the other and stuffing a hand into his pocket. "You would do that?"

She could see the playfulness in his eyes. He was calling her bluff, and she couldn't let it happen. "I just might. Maybe we'll ask all of the bachelors in town."

"So, what you're saying is, you think I'll bring in a lot of money?" He flashed her a wicked grin, and she punched him in the shoulder.

"I didn't say that." She turned and walked down the hall, heading out the front door. She could sense Colton behind her and turned to glance at him quickly before increasing her pace.

"Are there really that many single guys here? I thought you said the chances of dating were slim for a single girl."

She stopped abruptly and turned to him, causing him to sidestep to avoid tumbling into her. "I thought you were the one who had done all the studies on our community's ages."

Several older couples shuffled by in front of the fountain. Colton raised an eyebrow and motioned toward them. "Are you really going to argue that?"

"Okay, there are a lot of old people here, but there are also a lot of single people here as well. They just don't come out to events as often."

"Well, if the other older ladies are anything like Mrs. McCready, I can understand why."

Becca stared at him. "What do you mean by that?"

"I mean, they ask about your relationship status and then want to set you up with every Sally Sue and Rhonda Jo. I've had my fair share of blind dates, and it all starts with some older ladies meddling."

Becca took two steps forward, tilting her head back so she could look Colton in the face. "So, what you're saying is, you're in need of a date."

"Yeah, with you. You want to get some dinner?"

Oh, he was good. She couldn't feel her legs as they'd started to go wobbly under his gaze.

"I could use some food," she whispered.

He slipped his hand into hers, and she opened her eyes wide. "If you feel uncomfortable holding my hand in public, I understand. But all of these people are going to be talking about us hanging out together a lot anyway. Why not make it exciting for them?"

Shaking her head, Becca removed her hand from his and threaded it through his arm. When he gave her a confused expression, she said, "I like you, but I've had my heart broken before. Who knows where you'll be assigned in a few weeks."

"Slower is better than a complete stop, so I'll take it." His wide grin was like shooting off confetti in her chest. Her insides were having a royal party.

Two days later, it was Friday, a week before the festival, and Becca was still debating whether or not to have a bachelor auction. Sure, there were plenty of single ladies in town, but there might be some uproar at doing such a thing during a family event.

She had to decide by today to give everyone time to prepare if the theme was different, and she decided to walk out back, hoping the flowers would give her some inspiration.

The sight before her caused her to gasp, her thoughts swirling as she could see from the raised porch that the middle of the nursery had caved in. Her mind calculated the cost of the flowers inside the structure, knowing it would be devastating to her business if she lost everything.

She couldn't remember if she'd heard of wind or a major storm from the night before. The nursery was older but certainly not old enough to rot away, surely. It had been there since a few years after her parents had moved in, an anniversary gift for her mother built by her father.

Walking through the door, she went as far as she could, moving several potted plants to an area that hadn't collapsed.

She needed to get it fixed now, before it affected all the flowers in the small greenhouse. Pulling out her phone, she found Colton's phone number he'd typed into her phone the other night at dinner.

Answering after the first ring, his groggy voice said, "Hello?" Looking down at her watch, Becca felt guilty for the early morning wake-up call.

"Hey, sorry to bug you so early, but I was wondering if you can take a look at my nursery? One side caved in, and I'm worried the rest of it will do the same."

"Sure. Yeah. I'll be over in a few."

Walking around, she did her best to move the rest of the plants nearby, knowing Colton would need room to do whatever was necessary to fix it. A thrill ran through her at the thought that he was coming to her house and into such an intimate spot for her. But then again, she had several thousand dollars' worth of flowers growing in the enclosed space, and she couldn't risk losing them.

"Wow! I didn't know you have all this back here." His voice came from the door of the nursery, and she turned as he strode closer to her. "Let me take a look at this."

She stood back, admiring how the cut of his jeans fit just right and how when he pushed the beam up, the muscles in his back went taut. She could get used to this.

As Colton held the beam, the polycarbonate section fell to the ground. "Will you come hold this? I just need to get some tools so I can secure it again."

Becca hurried forward, using everything she had to not let the beam slip. She wasn't sure how he'd been able to move it with such ease. Keeping it in place was causing the muscles in her arms to burn, more than the random times she actually used weights to work out.

"Okay, I've got a ladder set up out here, and I'm just going to secure the main beam to the truss beams up here."

Becca felt a slight pressure pushing and pulling the beam into short changes of direction, and she hoped he'd hurry up before she dropped it on herself.

With a few quick screws, he called down to her, "Okay, you can let go now."

She heard the screwdriver again and worked to open her hands, as they were somewhat stuck in the shape of the beam after all the strain she'd put into it.

"Will you bring that square piece out? It looks like it just sits right on top of the boards."

Becca hefted the polycarbonate square, still feeling the soreness from helping with the flood clean-up a few days before. After angling to fit out the door, she walked around the structure and did her best to move it within Colton's reach. He grasped it with ease, moving the piece as though it weighed no more than a piece of paper. Dang, that was impressive.

Once he slid the piece into the slot, he stepped down the ladder, pulling the pins on the sides to close it up.

"You probably haven't had to use that since you've been here," Becca said, gesturing to the ladder.

"Actually, I used it at the McCready's last week. They were doing one of those stylish walls."

Becca motioned for him to follow her into the house. She walked up the stairs and into the kitchen through the back door, grateful she hadn't left a mess that morning. Pulling open the fridge, she asked, "Do you want juice or anything?"

"Milk?"

She pulled the light-blue-capped milk out of the fridge and set it on the counter, opening the cabinet to get a glass.

"Never mind. I'll be okay."

Frowning, Becca asked, "Huh?"

"If all you have is that watered-down stuff, I'll be fine for now." He pointed to her jug of 1% milk and turned up his nose.

Becca laughed. "I didn't know you were so picky about that kind of stuff. At least let me get you some water for coming out here." She tried to remember if she had any goodies in the pantry, but she hadn't been to the grocery store in quite some time.

"I'll take some water." He slid into a chair next to the small round table she used as a dining table, and for some reason, he looked so relaxed sitting there, like there was nowhere else he belonged.

Filling up a clear glass, she brought it over and sat it on the table in front of him. She pulled out the chair catty-corner from him and leaned her elbows on the table. For the most part, this guy was proving to be near perfect. But that niggled at Becca, making her wonder what he was hiding underneath.

Rationally, she knew there were guys different from Peter, but since the resemblance and profession were so close to her ex-fiancé, she couldn't help but wonder.

"You seem to be getting to know a lot of people in town. Would you ever stay?" She looked at her nails, too nervous to look him in the face.

"I do like it. I think I'm finally used to the dead-quiet at night, and that's helped me get some better sleep. But it's a fun little town with a lot of history, and I like that."

Cocking her head to the side, she asked, "Would you be willing to live here? After the subdivision, I mean."

He shrugged. "It would be a great place to live. I'd just have to figure out logistics with my job and getting things settled there."

At least he was being honest, even if it wasn't the concrete answer she was looking for.

He drained the glass within a few seconds and tapped the table. "Is there anything else I can fix while I'm here? I need to get going on those folding walls for Susie before she starts flipping out at me."

Becca smiled and stood, Colton doing the same. "Good luck with that. Hopefully it doesn't take you too long."

"I'm just hoping it will win me points in the 'win a date with the bachelor' you're organizing." He gave her his cockeye grin, and she hit him in the shoulder with the back of her hand.

"Oh, please. I don't even know if that's what we're going to do yet. Part of me thinks it would be a bad idea." She rolled her eyes and sighed, wishing she hadn't made the suggestion in the first place.

Colton breathed out in an exaggerated fashion. "You're just worried about some other girl bidding for me, aren't you?"

Becca hesitated, realizing how true his statement was. "Not at all. I just think some of the older ladies might be bored since they already have their men."

"Who's to say they won't bid too?"

Becca shook her head and rolled her eyes. "You're the worst. You know, I'll walk over to the rec center with you. I need to let Susie know about the fundraiser."

She might have left out the fact that she didn't want Susie near Colton for that long alone. And what else did she have to do but help? So much for giving up her spot as the organizer of the event.

CHAPTER 22

That night and the next morning seemed to pass in a flurry. Becca had worked for several hours helping Susie with odd jobs since her assistant still hadn't bothered to show her face. Then the morning and afternoon were spent at the flower shop, getting the flowers ordered and organizing the ones needed for the event. They were only a few days out, but it seemed like they were in a constant cycle of hurry up and wait.

A few days passed without seeing Colton, and while she might have been relieved of that fact at the beginning, she found her thoughts turning to him often. Several times she'd picked up her phone, thinking she heard her text message sound, her heart racing in the hopes that it was from him. But it was either her imagination or texts from someone else sending in orders.

She was in the shop, making a list of things she needed to get together for the raffle, when the bell above the door rang. Holding her breath, she moved to the front, hoping it was Colton. Instead, she saw a face she hadn't seen in a few months.

"Dani!" she squealed, rushing forward and wrapping her arms around her oldest and closest friend. "When did you get back?"

"About thirty minutes ago. My mom picked me up at the airport. I figured I needed to come see how things had progressed since our last phone call."

The mischievous look on the brunette's face caused Becca to roll her eyes. She stepped back and shook her head. "Not much has happened."

"You just touched your earlobe," Danielle said, pointing out the small action Becca did without thinking. "Spill, girl."

"Well, there was a flood of the town," Becca started slowly.

Danielle nodded. "That I know all about. I want to know about this stranger you've had to deal with quite a bit."

"He's tall, dark hair, brown eyes, a small scar on his chin from climbing a tree when he was younger."

With a face of surprise, Danielle said, "So, it's progressed further than I thought." She clapped her hands together before saying, "Have you kissed?"

Becca's cheeks burned almost instantly, and she turned, walking into the back room with footsteps close behind her.

"You have! And? How was it?"

Slumping into a chair near one of the tables, Becca put her head into her hands. "It was amazing. Like fireworks-shooting-off-in-the-background good. But I haven't seen or heard from him in a few days, which is odd because he was always around when I didn't want him to be, and now he's not around when I actually want him here."

A scraping sound caused her to look up as Danielle pulled a chair over next to her. "You'll be fine, Becca. My mom said she's met him a few times and he's a nice guy. And he was instrumental in helping out during the flood."

"Yeah, but Susie has her hooks in him; I can tell."

"I doubt it, Becca. I mean, I haven't met the guy yet, but he kissed you, right? He doesn't sound like the kind of guy who'd go kissing every single woman in town."

Becca let that sink in for several seconds. "You know how Susie is. She's got flirting down to a science. And he's either been avoiding me or inexplicably busy with something. If he really has feelings for me, he'd have at least texted or called, right? I had a gut feeling when he first started talking to me that he was trying to sway my vote. And now I think my instincts were right."

"Just because your ex-fiancé ran off with some other girl doesn't mean that this guy with the same profession is going to do the same." Danielle's words were more firm, and Becca could tell her patience was wearing thin. "And who knows? Maybe that was his original intention but now he's changed his mind."

She didn't want to talk about it anymore, feeling more frustrated as she turned over each of the interactions she'd had with Colton since he'd come to town. Had it all been an act? The thought fueled her anger, but after all the research she'd done about the subdivision, she knew the town needed the boost, especially after everything that had happened with the flood. She could vote yes for it to go through but she wasn't going to subject her heart to any more pain.

Changing the subject, she asked, "What about you? Did you meet any attractive foreign men on your trip?"

"None to write home about. But next time I take a trip like that, I'm dragging you along, even if I have to do so literally." Danielle grinned at her, the quiet confidence settling over Becca.

Becca had always been more outspoken than Danielle, but she wished she could have that one trait, the one where Danielle made the person next to her feel like the most important person in the world.

Her thoughts turned to Colton again, and something about his sudden absence made her wish she'd been able to block herself from the slippery slide of feelings for him. Because now, looking back, there were so many times when Peter claimed to be working late at the office, meeting with a client or getting stuck in traffic on the way back to Sage Creek, meaning he had to stay in the city. She'd been so grateful for Danielle's investigative skills, which helped Becca feel some kind of closure from the total silence she'd gotten from Peter.

She'd just have to wait and see. If she got worried about something now, she might blow it out of proportion.

CHAPTER 23

Colton was more than excited about the festival coming up. The results had come in for the water and ground tests after just a week, and the council had called a special meeting and voted Wednesday night for the subdivision to go through, Becca being one of the votes.

He'd tried to talk to her before and after the meeting but had been detained by several people asking about the details of the housing units. She slipped out before he could say anything.

Opening his phone, Colton sent a text message to Becca.

I didn't get a chance to talk to you tonight. Are you up for a shake at the diner?

He sat on the bench in front of the Town Hall fountain, staring at his screen in the hopes that she would respond just as quickly. Several minutes went by with no answer, and a sliver of fear slithered into his chest. After all they'd been through together in the past few weeks, had he read things wrong?

I know I've been MIA for the last few days. I've been working on a few things for the festival, and I can't wait for you to see them.

Reflecting back to their kiss by the pond, he relived it and noted that she hadn't squirmed away from him. She'd wanted the kiss just as much as he had.

He thought about the festival. He'd spent several hours working on the bifold walls Susie had requested, as well as a few more on something special just for Becca. Maybe she was hurt that he hadn't been around for so many days. Time had flown faster than he'd realized. He just hoped he hadn't been overthinking her feelings as well.

He dialed her number, hoping she'd pick up. Instead, the call went to her voicemail, and a pit formed in his stomach. An uneasy feeling came over him, and he wasn't sure how to fix it.

Checking the last text he'd sent her before tonight, he realized it had been several days since he'd talked to her. Blowing out a breath, he ran his hand through his hair. He just hoped she'd realize why he'd been missing when she saw what he'd built for her.

*B*ecca felt the exhaustion through her body as the day of the festival wore on. She'd been working to arrange all the flowers for most of the morning in the rec center and then made sure all the raffle items had been collected.

Her phone buzzed again, another message from Colton pleading for her to answer. He'd sent several over the last two days, as well as calling and leaving voicemails. But she'd stopped reading and listening after the first few.

As soon as she'd shown a change in her opinion to approve the subdivision after the flood, Colton had quit calling, texting, and coming by. Okay, maybe it had been a few days but before that, she couldn't shake him if she wanted. He'd done it. She'd fallen for him, and he'd gotten his vote and his project manager job, and then he was done with her, just like Peter. She knew better and still fell for him.

Becca thought they'd really connected, making his silence and absence cut deep. She didn't know why he'd started trying to contact her again, but she couldn't keep putting herself out there.

She deleted the message before reading it, knowing it was better to steel herself now rather than let things continue between the two of them. She just couldn't handle the heartbreak, and if she broke things off now, she hoped the wounds she already had would heal with her avoiding him.

"That birdhouse is beautiful. Who brought it in?" she asked Danielle, who she'd roped into helping her.

Danielle shrugged. "I'm not sure. It was here when I walked in earlier. It's amazing, though. Who do you think made it?"

Becca thought through several of the older men in town, the ones who'd taken up woodworking once they'd retired. She could leave Mr. McCready out since he'd gotten Colton to do most of the repairs on his house since Colton had been in town.

A few other people came in, bringing their items and leaving them on the table.

"Thank you all for helping out with this," Becca said, greeting each of them as they left. There had been a parade earlier, and several booths were in the park just outside the rec center, many of the townspeople taking up their usual spots with their concessions and crafts.

By the time they had the final raffle items, Becca was ready to get started and get this over with. For some reason, seeing glimpses of Colton around the townspeople made her feel like she'd been chained with this raffle she'd come up with.

Soon enough, the chairs were filled in the rec center, and the short historical production of the history of the festival played out on the stage. Then it was her turn.

"Good evening, everyone. Thank you for coming out and supporting us with this raffle. You'll see the table over here to my left is overflowing with items, and all of the money raised will be used to get a more efficient system to prevent flooding of the pond in the future, as well as help those with large bills from any damage sustained."

The crowd clapped, and Becca waited for it to die down before signaling Danielle. She brought up the first item, a set of kitchen towels, oven mitt, and napkins, all with the same pattern. With the amount of color and flowers, it had to have been made by Dixie Flores.

An hour passed by, the table clearing little by little. She was amazed by the generosity of the members of the town, and they'd met their goal by that point.

"Let's take a break, and we'll continue the raffle. Susie has made sure we have plenty of food there at the back, so go get some, relax, and come back to finish out the raffle."

The crowd moved quickly to form a line past the walls Colton had created, the chatter rising to loud volumes.

"Another great idea executed by the amazing Becca Taylor," Danielle said, stepping back on stage and giving her a hug. "What a great way to help out the town."

"We've still got a lot to raffle off, though." She looked at several of the items, feeling even more tired. Speaking in front of people didn't make her super nervous, but the extended amount she'd already done had zapped the little bit of energy she had left.

Danielle leaned in close. "Better go find your boy Colton. Isn't there some kind of dance tonight?"

Becca frowned, searching the crowd for him. He stood near the door, surrounded by several women, and he appeared to be entertaining them. Maybe that's what he'd been doing during his silence.

Fury sparked inside her. Had none of their time together meant anything to him? And that kiss. She'd felt the sparks between them, but was it possible it was only on her end? She couldn't believe he could be so two-faced to have wooed her for her vote.

And now he was flirting with half the single women in town, from ages twenty to forty-five.

"I've got a major headache coming on, Dani. Can you take care of this?" Becca asked, motioning toward the table.

Danielle's eyes looked over the crowd and seemed to see what Becca had already noted. "Becca, you'll be fine. Talking to him is a better option than assuming."

"That's not why I'm going home," Becca said, stamping a foot with the last three words.

"Okay," Danielle said, taking a step back with her hands raised. "I've got this. You go rest. But promise me you'll talk to him tomorrow."

The intensity of Danielle's gaze bore through her, and Becca turned so she didn't have to look her in the eyes as she lied. "Fine. Tomorrow."

Keeping her eyes on Colton, she moved through the crowd, making sure he couldn't see her escape. She didn't need him running after her if he, in fact, did care about her at all.

Colton loved the excitement of the town throughout the festival, from the parade to the fried foods to the buzz of the townspeople. He knew quite a few of them now, and he felt more at home than he had in forever. This was the kind of place where he could see himself for the rest of his life, hopefully convincing his mother to move closer.

But what he wanted most was Becca right there next to him, building a home together, a family, a life. He could feel it in the depths of his soul, as if taking the first sip of water after a long drought.

She'd been busy on the stage, flitting about and getting things ready for the raffle when he came in, and he knew he'd need her full attention if he was going to apologize properly. Hopefully, he'd catch her after all the prizes were gone and she could really hear what he had to say.

Maybe he'd even do it publicly once she raffled off the birdhouse he'd built for her. He'd planned to raise the price during the auction with the help of several of the older people. He just hoped his plan would work out and she'd trust him.

He'd watched her vibrance for life as she got excited for each of the prizes to be raffled. There was just so much about her that surprised him. The trauma she'd been through still weighed on her, but she also showed him how comfortable she was in Sage Creek.

Once they were dismissed to get food, Colton heard his stomach rumble and walked over to get in line. Within seconds, he was surrounded by several ladies he'd met during his few weeks there.

"Congrats on the subdivision going through, Colton," one woman to his right said, stroking her fingers up and down his arm. He couldn't remember her name, but he took a step back, hoping to get her to drop her arm.

"What's going on with you and Becca?" Tara Jones asked. She looked more curious than anything, and Colton was grateful for at least one girl who wasn't trying to fawn over him while in line.

Colton opened his mouth to speak, but before he could respond, the first woman giggled, sounding more like a cackle.

"Becca dating anyone after that Greek God, Peter Hamburg? I doubt it. The man had everything going for him. Looks and an amazing job with tons of money coming in. He was the picture of the perfect boyfriend." The woman smacked her lips together, rubbing the lipstick around.

Tara turned to her, her arms folded. "I think she dodged a bullet. The guy was a tool who changed completely once he got a raise. Becca deserves better."

The line moved forward, and the conversation around him changed, leaving him with the words spinning around his head. He couldn't get the words "picture perfect boyfriend" out of his head. Was that what Becca wanted? She seemed like a woman who didn't care much about money, but then again, she'd agreed to marry Peter. Would getting a promotion turn Colton into someone similar to her ex-fiancé?

He wished the subdivision hadn't gone through. Then he wouldn't be stuck here, pining for a woman who was obviously trying to avoid him. She'd never returned his calls or texts, and when he tried to stop by her shop, she'd sent out her young employee instead. Maybe it was for the best that he head out and leave her to her security.

Casting a quick glance at the stage when a voice came through on the microphone, he noticed Becca's absence. The woman speaking was Becca's best friend, Danielle, and she announced they would start the raffle again in about ten minutes.

Deciding to get some food later, he excused himself from the group and walked to the platform.

"Did Becca leave?" he asked the woman, not even pausing for a hello.

The sadness in Danielle's eyes told him all he needed to know. "Yeah, she said she wasn't feeling well. Can I give her a message?"

Shaking his head, Colton's chest tightened like it was about to implode. The conversation he'd had with the women in line swirled through his thoughts. He'd been lying to himself the entire time.

He walked across the block and down Main Street in the crisp spring air. The stars were bright here, especially against the dark sky, and Colton already felt the loss of the daydreams he'd built up as his future here.

He could see Becca's home from where he stood on the corner by the doctor's office, across the street from her flower shop. Seeing one light on upstairs, he debated whether or not to knock on her door.

Covering the distance in a matter of seconds, he knocked, or more like pounded on the door.

"Becca! Becca! Danielle said you went home. Please just open the door and talk to me. Tell me why you won't talk to me, and I'll leave you alone." He knocked again before saying, "I like you, Becca, and I want us to be together. But I can't do that if there's always a wall between us."

He heard a sound relatively close to the door, and he moved over to the window, feeling a bit like a stalker as he cupped both hands around his eyes and tried to peer in. A large cat was lounging next to a half-eaten sandwich on the side table. The television was on, but there was no sign of Becca.

As the emotions warred within him, he turned and walked to the hotel, figuring now was the best time to get on with his life. He couldn't stay in this town a moment longer, knowing the woman he loved wouldn't speak to him and wouldn't even tell him why. Best to save himself the embarrassment before it was laid out for him.

* * *

It took an eternity for Monday morning to roll around, and once inside his boss's office, he explained how he needed to be moved back to one of the finish crews.

"You want off the job? This is what you've been working for, Colton. Are you sure that's really what you want to do?" Adam paced back and forth in his luxurious office.

Colton shifted back in the wingback chair, blowing out a breath. "I'm not sure I'm cut out to be a project manager, Adam."

"I know I don't say much," Adam said, pulling something from his desk. "But I think the world of you, man. You're the most qualified person in our company. You've even taught me everything I know about residential building since I got this assignment."

"Thank you, sir. Maybe a bit more time with the finish crew will help me prepare a bit more. I just don't want to let the company down," Colton said, moving his eyes to the decorative rug. More so, he didn't want to let himself down. He didn't know another job but being the carpenter, and if it was going to change him, he didn't want a part of it. He might be dooming himself to a life of bachelorhood, but he could live with himself the way he was. It seemed like the hole in his heart would never heal anyway. It was better to keep his hands busy with all the little things that came with building rather than having to actually think about how he'd messed things up with Becca.

"I'll put our new guy, Peter, on it for now, but if you change your mind, it's still yours."

Colton stood, reaching his hand over the large desk between him and his boss. "Thank you, sir. I'll let you know if anything changes."

He walked out of the office, letting out a deep breath. He thought he'd feel relieved and things would go back to normal, but instead, his mind conjured up a picture of the beautiful girl with hazel eyes he'd left in Sage Creek. He'd do everything he could to avoid hurting her. And this was the sacrifice.

CHAPTER 26

"Becca, you need to smile once in a while. People are talking about how the flowers are wilting faster because the flower girl isn't her usual happy self." Velda set a plate overflowing with a sandwich and French fries on the counter, glaring at Becca.

"I smile," Becca said, frowning.

"She's sulking," Danielle said, sliding next to Becca and stealing one of her fries.

The older woman behind the counter leaned forward, looking excited for any snippet of information.

"I don't sulk. I'm just here to eat my sandwich in peace." Becca picked up a section of the turkey club, taking a bite from it so she didn't have to speak anymore.

Danielle turned to Velda and lowered her voice, still keeping it loud enough for Becca to hear. "She's in love with Colton Maxfield, but she's too stubborn to tell him. I've told her I'll drive her to Denver and help her find him, but she refuses."

"I'm still here, you two." Becca bit down on a fry, feeling more sour than she had when she walked in.

She'd thought about Colton more over the past week than she had while he was here, which was a lot. Why would he leave without saying goodbye? She'd only heard on Monday that he'd gone, when it was all around town that he left the morning after the festival. The feeling of betrayal she'd felt after finding out Peter had ditched her on her wedding day was at least double now, knowing he'd just left without saying a word. Especially when he knew she'd been left before.

He'd used her, getting close to her to get her vote, and then he'd vanished.

Danielle had already been over it with her several times, and it sounded like she was on her soapbox again. "You didn't text him back. That means you have to be the one to show him how much he means to you. Like doing something out of your *comfort zone*." Her best friend emphasized the last two words slowly and with emphasis.

"If he really cared about me, he wouldn't have left without a note or a word."

Danielle scoffed next to her. "Really? I remember you saying he came over and pounded on your door, wanting to talk. And you didn't. open. the. door."

"Relationships go two ways, honey," Velda said, one hand on her hip. "I'd say the ball's in your court."

"Days without speaking to me after we'd spent several days in a row together. Doesn't that sound a lot like Peter to you?"

Danielle shook her head. "Yeah, but Peter never apologized or went out of his way to make it up to you. And I'm pretty sure he has a good reason for his radio silence those few days. But have you let him explain that to you? No. At least hear him out before you give up completely."

Velda moved to help another customer, and Danielle ate

her food in silence. But the feeling of guilt started to overtake Becca.

What would her life look like with Colton in it on a more permanent basis? And what would it be like without him there? Empty. That's how it would be.

"Fine. I'll go if you drive." Becca pulled some cash from her purse and left it on the counter. Standing, she turned to Danielle, who looked at her with eyes wide, her mouth hung open.

"Are you serious?" Danielle asked, swallowing harder than looked comfortable.

"If we don't go now, I'll probably back out." Becca turned and walked to the door, turning slightly to see her friend scramble from her place at the bar.

"Velda, I'll pay for this once I get back from Denver!" Danielle let out a squeal, turning the heads of the rest of the patrons in the restaurant.

The older woman waved her hand. "It's on the house. Just make sure that girl comes back with a man." She smiled wide, pointing in Becca's direction. That was all she needed, the whole town talking about her love life once again.

Not that any of it was certain right then, but a spark of hope flared. Maybe if she begged forgiveness, she'd know how Colton really felt about her. Because she loved him, loved that he was willing to put himself into the throes of helping a town he barely knew for only a few days.

But more than that, she loved how he made her feel safe, that he'd try new things like helping her at the flower shop. And the way her body nearly sang when he kissed her, it was a sensation she'd probably never feel again if she didn't go after him.

The two of them piled into Danielle's crossover vehicle, and as they clicked on their seatbelts, Danielle looked over, her eyebrows raised nearly to her hairline.

"You're sure about this? I don't want to get in an accident because you have a freak-out session."

"I'll be fine. I just need to breathe. We're not going into Salt Lake either, so I think that will help."

Danielle pulled out of the driveway, down Main Street, and onto the main highway. The familiar tightening in her stomach began the faster Danielle drove, getting closer and closer to the county-line sign.

Blowing out quick breaths, Becca grabbed onto the handle of the door, squeezing as hard as she could. She was leaving her safe zone, and the thought of it scared her more than she wanted to admit. But if she kept her mind on Colton, on finding out if he felt the same emptiness without her that she did without him, maybe she'd make it out of one of her fears alive.

She saw the sign to the right and sucked in a breath, tightening every muscle in her body as the car sped over the invisible line between counties. The breath stayed locked in her lungs for several moments, and for a split second, she wondered if any of this was worth it.

Minutes ticked by, and the exhaustion of her tension caused her to relax a bit. Danielle drove, dancing to each song as it came on the radio. She chatted every once in a while, but Becca didn't feel like talking as she watched the ground pass under the car bit by bit.

The four-hour drive passed like days, but Danielle finally pointed to Becca. "Look up Dream Homes on the maps app. I'd prefer to not get lost here."

Becca responded, feeling like each movement was robotic. The excitement that she'd actually broken free of her county had worn off, and she felt the anxiety of the leap she was taking.

Once parked outside a large high-rise, Becca walked inside, asking for Colton at the front desk.

"He isn't here at the moment. Is there someone I can get to help you?"

Becca fidgeted with a strand of hair. "He said his boss is Adam?"

"Adam Summers? That's the main boss of Dream Homes. I'm not sure he'll see you without an appointment."

Her hopes fell. She'd wanted to take Colton by surprise, to see in his face whether he was happy to see her or that he felt nothing for her.

"Who won't I see without an appointment?" a man asked, coming from the elevators behind the desk.

The receptionist nodded. "Good afternoon, Mr. Summers. This young lady is looking for Colton Maxfield."

The man turned his attention to Becca, looking her up and down with a gaze that made her uncomfortable. "You wouldn't happen to be the florist from Sage Creek, would you?"

A slight hope took in her, and she nodded. "Yes, Becca Taylor. I was hoping to find Colton here. I have a few things I didn't get to say to him and made the trek here to do so." Her last few words tumbled out of her mouth, her tongue dry.

"You just missed him about an hour ago. He came back and said he wanted to be back on the job in your small town. Something about a flower girl he loved."

Her brain spun. He loved her, even though she'd ghosted him for the past couple of weeks?

"Did you take him off the project?" She was trying so hard not to let the tears fall that her voice quivered as she spoke.

Adam shook his head. "No, Colton asked to be taken off when he came back almost a week ago. But then he came in today, saying how he'd made a mistake and needed to go back. Something about the lumber guy from your town saying how much he was missed."

Tanner Hart. How had the two of them connected in Denver?

"So, he's on his way back to Sage Creek?" Becca's mind was muddled with all the information it was trying to process. She wondered if Colton had actually used the words love or if that was something Adam had added.

"Yep. He's not too far ahead of you." Adam pointed to the door as if Becca could see him right outside.

Just before she turned to look out the door, a familiar build stepped up behind.

"Hey, Adam, I was going over these—" Peter's face was focused on a stack of papers in his hands, and when he looked up and saw Becca, he stopped in his tracks. "What are you doing here?" he asked, the look on his face a mixture of shock and embarrassment.

The tears she'd felt moments before evaporated, and tipping up her chin, she said, "I'm looking for the man I love."

Before he could say anything, she continued, "And no, he's not you." Taking a step forward, she took an open palm to Peter's face, giving it all the feelings she'd gone through since that day eighteen months ago.

His hand reached up to his cheek, and the redness spread to the rest of his face.

"That's for not having the decency to tell me we were done to my face. To be honest, you leaving me was probably the best thing that's ever happened."

She turned to Adam, keeping her smile under wraps as she saw his look of surprise. "Thank you so much for your help." She ran out the door and down the road, retracing her steps back to Danielle's car.

"We have to go," she said, breathless as she slipped into the passenger seat.

"What do you mean? Did you talk to him?" Danielle asked, turning the key in the ignition.

Becca shook her head. "He's heading back to Sage Creek. Drive!" After a few minutes of fiddling with her fingers, she said, "Peter works for Colton's company."

Danielle turned wide eyes her way, her mouth open in shock. "No way. When I looked into him, he was at another company."

With a quick shrug, Becca shook her head. "He was there, behind Adam, the boss."

"What did you do? Please tell me you told him off!" Danielle adjusted her grip on the steering wheel, looking more excited than she had when Becca said she wanted to leave Sage Creek for Denver.

"I slapped him across the face there in the lobby. You should have seen how surprised he was." With a thin smile, she relived the small moment of triumph after waiting eighteen months.

"I would've paid to see that."

The drive back seemed to take longer, and with each white truck they approached, Becca turned her head to look inside, hoping to see the face of the man she loved.

They didn't see him on the drive, and when they pulled onto Main Street in Sage Creek, Becca's eyes darted up and down the street, looking for his truck. Danielle slowed down so they could look both ways on each street they passed.

It wasn't until they made it to Becca's street that she spotted the green truck, parked outside her house. She opened the door before Danielle had come to a complete stop, hearing a loud hammering sound.

She followed it around the side of the house and saw the source. Colton was standing in the middle of her open flower garden in the back corner, working the ornate birdhouse she'd seen at the festival into the ground.

"What are you doing?" she asked, trying her best to keep from showing emotion.

Colton jumped and turned her direction. He looked guilty and gave her a hesitant smile. "I thought I'd get this put into your garden where it belongs."

Taking a few steps forward, Becca asked, "What do you mean? I thought the mayor purchased the birdhouse from the raffle."

"I might have asked him to. I knew you wouldn't be bidding on the items you were auctioning off, and I made this with you in mind." He ran his hand up the side of the birdhouse and tapped on it.

Becca closed the distance, leaving about a foot between the two of them. She pointed up to the feeder. "You made this for me? Why?"

Colton glanced at the ground, his jaw working back and forth. "I just wanted to show you how much I cared about you."

She couldn't help but let the corner of her mouth turn up a bit. "And you showed that real well by disappearing on me and going back to Denver after you got my vote."

His mouth opened and quivered a bit, his hands raised as if to help him think. "That was a mistake I wish I could take back. I tried to stop by your house the night of the festival and talk to you, but I was too late. You'd already shut me out. I should've tried harder, but I might have felt like I wasn't worthy of you after hearing a description of your ex-fiancé."

"You were worried about a piece of scum like Peter?"

He took in a deep breath. "Everyone said he was different after he got his promotion. I was worried about hurting you like he did."

Becca reached out for him, slipping her hand in his. "Colton, there are some similarities between the two of you, but the differences are where it counts. Peter would have never helped out a flooding town, nor would he have made the effort to get to know a bunch of townsfolk who he might or might not see again. And he definitely wouldn't have taken the time to make something as special as this just for me." She motioned to the birdhouse, her chest squeezing a little at the effort he'd put into the little green two-story creation.

She squeezed his hand and smiled. "Colton, I love you for the man you are. I don't worry about you changing like him because you've already got your head on straight."

He shook his head, his foot moving back and forth in the soft dirt at their feet.

She reached forward and tipped his chin up with her pointer finger, swallowing as she looked into his eyes. "I'm sorry I didn't respond to your texts and calls and avoided you. I felt like you'd already started pulling away from me, and I knew I wouldn't make it through another heartbreak. And when I saw all those women around you at the festival, I ran."

"I promise I was just working on the walls and birdhouse, and every time I went to text or call you, it was really late. It won't happen again. Those women came to me unprompted, unfortunately. You're the only one I want."

"I'm sorry I assumed. You'll never believe it, but Danielle just drove me to Denver and back." She chewed on her bottom lip, waiting for his response.

His eyes went wide, his mouth open in a half-believing smile. "Why did you do that?"

"Because I love you, and when you love someone, it's worth it to get out of your comfort zone to show that person how much they mean to you. I really screwed things up between us, and I wanted to fix them, in person."

He pulled her toward him, his strong arms holding her against his chest. She slid her arms around his waist, leaning her head on his chest as she glanced up at the birdhouse. "It's beautiful."

"You're beautiful," he said, catching Becca's attention. "I can't believe you crossed the county line…for me."

She glanced up, and he moved a section of hair away from her eyes, the softness of his touch causing shivers to ripple through her body. "I love you too. I think I was so scared you would leave me heartbroken that I ran. But I'm done running. I'm here to stay, if you'll have me."

Her brain went blank, and she did the only thing she could think of to remedy the situation. She moved on tiptoe and pulled him down enough to press her lips to his, feeling like she'd entered her dreams and they were finally being fulfilled.

"I'll go where you go, Colton Maxfield."

EPILOGUE

The fall weather brought the smell of leaves, and Becca grinned as she hiked up to the pond after working at the flower shop. Colton had texted for her to meet him there, and she was excited for some time by the place she loved the most. It would be winter soon enough, and even though it was pretty with all the white and the frozen water, there was something about the autumn leaves that had her remembering all the times her mother had taken her there.

At the top of the hill, she noticed several flower petals along the ground, looking to have come from several different flowers. She tried to see where the path led, but it passed by the pond, and she couldn't see anything from there.

She followed the trail, going through the orders from that day. There wasn't any certain order that contained each of these flowers all together. How did he get these?

With a grin, she moved along the path, taking in the beauty of the vibrant red, orange, and yellow leaves mixed in with the dark green pines.

As she came around the bend, she saw a blanket with a picnic basket atop it and Colton grinning up at her.

"How did you do this?" she asked, gesturing back to the petals on the ground.

He shrugged. "It took a little bit of planning. Are you hungry?"

"Yes," she said, almost in harmony with the growl of her stomach. She sat down, taking a small container of berries from him. She noticed his hand shook a bit, and she studied his face. "Are you all right?"

"Uh, yes. Why?"

"Because you're acting a bit strange. And this is quite the setup for a simple date night out."

Colton's eyes widened, and he looked like the breath had left him completely. He turned, pulling something out of the basket. Moving to one knee, he said, "I was going to wait until after lunch, but I might not be able to get through it if I wait any longer."

Becca felt light-headed, like she'd been through a world of emotions in only a few seconds.

"I love you, Rebecca Jane Taylor. I know we've gone through a lot, and I want you by my side for the rest of forever. Will you marry me?"

A single tear ran down her cheek, and she nodded. "Yes, I will." She wrapped her arms around him, pulling his lips to hers. "There's no one I'd rather spend my life with than you."

* * *

Keep reading for a sneak peak of Danielle and Liam's story in
Love Under Review

* * *

Thank you for reading *Love Under Construction!* If you enjoyed it, I would love to see a review from you. You can also subscribe to Britney's newsletter here:
Subscribe to Britney's List
Or join her Facebook Reader Group

CHAPTER 1

DANIELLE

*L*iam Pearson watched the sunrise from the front porch, breathing in the fall morning air. After a long day at the hospital in Grand Junction, Colorado, the day before, it was nice to sit on something other than hard waiting room chairs, especially after trying to keep Cari occupied as her mother went in for surgery.

He'd had to fight his six-year-old niece to get in the car to go home late that night. An image of her defiance played in his mind, and he smiled, realizing she was the spitting image of her mother when she did that. Cari had been lying on the hospital bed next to her mother, playing a game on his tablet. He understood somewhat the fear the young girl harbored. She'd gone through so much in her young life, and the hospital was a place of unknowns. Would her mother come back home alive after her treatments? Because her father hadn't after his car accident.

At this hour, he should be waking her up to get ready for school, but he needed the silence, the quiet reflection this moment gave him. He'd never had moments like these in

New York, and he wondered how he'd made it five years there without slowing down even a bit.

Every day over the past six months, his decision to leave investment banking and move in with his sister and niece in Sage Creek, Colorado, proved to be a good move, and better health was only the tip of the iceberg. Had someone told him he'd now own an independent bookstore, he'd have thought they'd lost a few brain cells.

Most of the stress he felt now was in regard to his sister's health. She'd been diagnosed with leiomyosarcoma the month before, after several months of fatigue, nausea, and weight loss. As stubborn as Kara Plumfield was, it had taken her fainting and blacking out on two separate occasions to convince her she needed to get checked out. But Liam hadn't imagined the whirlwind that would come of it.

They'd had to wait for the specialist to come over from Denver. The surgery from the day before had been to remove the tumor in her stomach, a procedure with several risks. But Kara had never wavered, knowing she had to do whatever she could to prolong time with her daughter.

On the doctor's recommendation, Kara had chosen to do a session of radiation before they sewed her back up. Liam just hoped it would get all of the cancerous cells and help his sister get back to her normal vivacious personality. She still gave off as much enthusiasm as she could from her hospital bed, but that spark of excitement seemed to wane each time she saw the doctor.

The door opened, and Cari walked out, her hair sticking out in every direction. She rubbed her eyes beneath her glasses and climbed into his lap, snuggling her head against his chest. For the moment, all was right with the world, and he could have stayed like that for days. He'd checked his phone several times in the half-hour since he'd been awake, knowing this morning's updates would bring critical information about his sister's health.

"How'd you sleep?" he whispered into Cari's ear.

"Okay. I had one bad dream that woke me up. But I closed my eyes and went back to sleep."

Liam smiled, kissing the top of her head. He could only imagine what she would dream about. Most likely hospitals and needles as she'd seen the nurses poke and prod her mother for blood samples over the past few weeks.

"How about pancakes for breakfast? I'll get making them while you get ready for school. How does that sound?" He leaned back and smiled as her head popped up, eyes wide.

"Can we call my mom?" Her eyelashes fluttered, and as much as Liam wanted to call his sister, he knew she still needed the rest.

He shook his head. "Your mommy's probably really tired still from the surgery yesterday. When I hear back from the hospital, we'll know we can call her. Maybe after school. Is that okay?" He watched as the sadness on her face disappeared with his proposal.

"Can I wear my purple dress?" Cari asked, bouncing up and down on his knee.

Liam turned his lips to the side and tapped his cheek with one finger, watching as she waited in suspense. "It looks like it will be a nice day. I think your purple dress would be fine."

She slid off his lap and danced on her toes in celebration before running inside. Her footsteps pounded up the stairs, the sound echoing through the hallway and out the front door.

Liam looked out at the line of trees over the tops of the houses across the street and smiled. She definitely got her zest for life from her mother.

Walking in, Liam pulled out the bag of pancake mix and measured it out, not needing to look at the directions anymore after the many times he'd made them over the past few months. He looked around the kitchen, seeing his sister's touch everywhere. Her favorite color was plum, and some of the appliances she owned were either completely that color or they had some part in that shade.

A minute or two later, Cari ran down the stairs and took up her usual seat at the table. Liam studied her face as she stared at the griddle, her eyes wide with excitement. He'd never met anyone who loved pancakes more than his niece.

He tried to hide a smile as his eyes traveled to her hair. It looked as though she'd tried to put it into a ponytail, but with the large bumps on top and several sections sticking out on the sides, she looked like she'd been in a tussle rather than just waking up.

"Here are a few hot off the griddle," he said with a smile, piling two pancakes on a paper plate. He poured syrup over the top of it and gave her a fork. "When you're done, we'll have to do something with your hair."

Cari turned to him with a scowl. "I already did it."

"I just want to fix one little part," Liam said, making a small space in between his forefinger and thumb.

Cari liked being independent, especially with her clothes and hair. Liam wasn't all that good at the fancy hair Kara could create with a few elastic bands, but he'd learned fast how to braid and use bows to his advantage.

"Fine. But we get to go to the park after school today if I let you." She held out her fork, using it to emphasize each word. Her negotiation skills were something to admire.

Liam chuckled, the serious face of his niece reminding him so much of Kara when they were younger. She was three years older than him and should have the world ahead of her. He just hoped the results of the surgery would be favorable and they could get back to their lives.

Twenty minutes later, they were out the door and walking the few blocks to Sage Creek elementary school.

"Don't forget. We're going to the park after school," Cari said, her lips pursed and her chin raised.

"If it doesn't rain, we will."

She folded her arms against her chest. "You said we could go to the park. I think we should go even in the rain."

Raising both hands in surrender, Liam chuckled. "We'll see what we can do."

Cari hesitated, and Liam could tell the wheels were turning from his statement. "If we don't go to the park, then you owe me a big bowl of ice cream."

"Deal." Liam pulled her into a hug, but she tore away and waved, disappearing into the crowd of children playing on the playground. Liam smiled, remembering when he'd do that with his own mother.

His thoughts turned to his mother as he walked back to the bookstore on Main Street. It was just south of the coffee shop, probably the best spot they could have hoped for as people would grab their beverage and walk over, looking for their latest read. It had been their mother's dream to own one, as she loved reading or anything that had to do with books. In his mind's eye, Liam could see her chatting away when he was as young as Cari, talking about how the characters in the book she was currently reading "moved" her.

It had been Kara's idea to open the store in Sage Creek, and while Liam had been skeptical that a bookstore would survive in a small town like this, he'd put up the money to get it started and trusted his sister that it would all work out. Five months in, every day he was surprised by how much income they were making and the number of people he spoke to about this book or that.

Now, New York seemed light-years away, as if that had been a long dream he'd had and this was what his reality looked like. He was content for the most part, aside from worrying about his sister. But he wouldn't have been able to help out like this, taking care of Cari and driving back and forth to Grand Junction for this appointment or that surgery, if he still lived across the country.

Opening the door to the bookstore, Liam flipped the lights on and walked to set his current book down on the counter. It was a mystery, one that many of the citizens of the town had already bought or borrowed. MK Malone was the hot topic for many, and Liam was pleasantly surprised when he'd finally broken down and started reading it.

He'd always thought cozy mysteries were for girls, as the main character was usually some snoopy woman who couldn't mind her own business. But the way the author had crafted the characters and the plot so far, Liam had to smile several times throughout the first half as he realized the author had linked with points A, B, and C from the beginning of the book. Such nuances he'd overlooked until they'd begun to come into play. He found himself looking forward to seeing how it ended.

He walked in the direction of the small breakroom in back, past the rows of shelves and the small study desks along the wall, to place his leftovers in the fridge for lunch before he moved to the large event room. He'd ordered several new computers to go next to the row of desks, and with all the little trinkets he'd started stocking, he'd drawn in more and more customers.

When looking for a place to open up shop, Kara had the idea to find something big enough for the books and space large enough to allow people to talk about them. After looking throughout Sage Creek and finding nothing suitable at first, Liam asked the landlord if they could rent two units and place a few doors in the wall that divided them to allow passage between the two. He'd approved without hesitation, glad to rent out both.

The bell over the door chimed, and Liam walked back to the counter to see who it was. "Oh, hey, Tanner." He walked over and shook the hand of the owner of the hardware store. They'd hung out quite a bit before his sister had taken a turn for the worse, but with the extra appointments and surgery, it had been a while since they'd gotten together. "What can I do for you today?"

"I'm just wondering if you have any books on sewing?"

Liam raised his eyebrow, curious as to why Tanner Hart would suddenly need something for sewing. He'd been the quarterback for his high school and had even gone to school on scholarship. Liam knew a lot of guys who could sew, but that was something he couldn't picture Tanner doing. "Yeah, here in the Arts and Crafts section."

They walked over to one of the back rows, and Liam waved across the selection that spanned several shelves.

Tanner's eyes went wide, and he frowned. "It's for my mother, so any advice you have would be great. She wanted one with embroidery. Is that when they make a whole bunch of x's on the white fabric?"

Liam laughed and slapped Tanner on the back. "Yep. Okay, here at the bottom, we have a lot of those kinds of books, different themes along here. If there isn't something you think she'd like, I can order one for you. When do you need it by?"

"Tomorrow," Tanner said, a sheepish grin on his face. He bent down and looked over the books displayed there, pulling out one with fairytale designs. "I'm going to go with this one. If she doesn't like it, I'll send her here and you can order her something."

Liam turned and walked back to the counter, realizing he

hadn't started the computer up just yet. "At least you thought about her the day before her birthday, right?"

"Yep." Tanner chuckled and pulled out his wallet, extending a credit card toward Liam. "What are you doing in a couple of weeks? A bunch of us were going to head up into the mountains on side-by-sides the weekend after Colton gets back from his honeymoon, and we haven't seen you in a while. You should come."

Focusing on the computer, Liam nodded, swiping the card through the reader. "It sounds like a lot of fun, but I've got Cari."

"No news yet about Kara?" Tanner's lips drooped, making him look ten years older. He was one of a handful of people in town who truly knew what was going on with Liam's sister. It was hard enough having his sister in the hospital, but in a town like this, Liam would get attacked by the questions and pity stares.

Aside from Tanner, Colton Maxfield, the builder of a new subdivision and one of the first people to welcome him in town, along with his fiancée, Becca, and two or three of the older ladies in town were about the only people who knew her condition. Becca owned the flower shop up Main Street, and the one time Liam had broken down and told Colton just after Kara's diagnosis, she'd sent several bouquets to the hospital.

"I've just been waiting for a call that Kara has woken up. And any news on her counts. It might be too early to know too much, but I'll take whatever information they'll give me. I'm hoping she can come home next week, but who knows."

Tanner signed his name on the touchscreen and replaced the pen. "What if I arrange for someone to watch Cari? Since it's fall, we won't have light for too long."

The idea was tempting, but Liam wasn't going to hold his breath. Tanner was a good-looking single guy. There wasn't a chance he'd actually remember to talk to someone about babysitting Tanner's niece once he walked out the door. At least, that would have been Liam's mentality just a few years ago.

"I mean, if you can find someone, then I'll see what I can do. It all depends on when Kara gets out and what she needs right now."

Tanner smiled. "Awesome. I'll get it all set up." He waved goodbye as he headed out with the book in hand.

Liam grinned, thinking of the fun it would be to adventure into the hills behind Sage Creek, something not possible in Manhattan. But then he remembered his sister and niece and brought himself back to reality. There was no way he was going to let either one of them down now, when they needed him most. He'd already done that to his sister once, and he wasn't about to repeat it.

Checking the time, he moved into action, knowing the weekly book club would be arriving in a couple of hours. It had become a tradition for a group of over a dozen ladies to stop in once a week to talk about the books they were reading. It was great for business and even for a good chuckle when Liam managed to catch snippets of the conversation.

When the seats were all arranged in the large room they used for bigger gatherings, Liam settled behind the counter. He settled in with the MK Malone book, intrigued as the clues came in for who had killed the town chef.

Things were quiet for the next two hours, and as he finished the last page, it felt like he'd just stepped out of a new world and into his regular one. A thought somewhat depressing.

He looked at the back cover, reading about the author, but the biography was only two sentences long and no picture.

The thought crossed his mind that he should contact the

author to do a reading and sign some books in the next month. They'd had two other authors visit since the store opened, which always helped sales go up as people flooded into the store. The book club wasn't the only group of people reading the cozy mysteries, and he couldn't keep the books in stock. That could be a big enough pull to draw the author into their sleepy little town.

The bell rang on the other side of the wall, and Liam jotted on a sticky note to find contact info on the author when he finished helping the book group settle in.

"Ah, Liam, dear. It's so good to see you again. How is your sister?" Mrs. McCready asked. She was a small woman, her hair looking like a snowfall around her shoulders. Reaching up, she patted his cheek as though he were still a small child. She reminded him of the grandparents he'd never met, having lost them when he was much younger than Cari.

Liam gave her a small smile. "I'm just waiting to hear how things turned out with the tests." He waved his cell phone as if it would summon the call from the hospital right then.

Mrs. McCready gasped. "I hope it was all clear. That would be such a wonderful miracle. Gordon has some more tests on Tuesday, so we'll be heading to Grand Junction then. Do let me know if I can bring Kara anything, will you?"

The McCreadys had found out about Kara's condition by accident, as Mr. McCready was taken in after some abnormalities in his bloodwork. Liam and Kara had just walked out of the doctor's office located in the hospital after getting the news of her condition, and the McCreadys had been there. In a way, it was comforting to share the burden with a couple who'd already felt like family since he'd moved to Sage Creek.

"Yes, ma'am." Liam moved to pick up a piece of paper on the floor. "Is there anything else I can get for you before your party arrives?"

"I don't think so, dear. Thank you for letting us use this room, as always. It's better than all of us trying to fit into each other's houses, I'll tell you that!"

With a smile, Liam said, "Anytime. I'll just be in the back if you need me. Today's shipment should be arriving at any moment, and I'll have a few extra copies of the book you're going to discuss."

He turned and strode away, hoping to avoid the rest of the ladies in the group as the door opened and the noise level increased. While they were all very nice, he could see them calculating ways to introduce him to the single ladies in their lives, and that wasn't something he wanted or needed right now. He was focused on taking care of his niece and keeping the bookstore running, in the hope that his sister would be back in his life, bossing him around like she always had. Relationships were sticky, and he'd learned enough from his last one to know he was better off making his own decisions.

Life was easier without the worry of losing someone he loved. He'd already done that three times, with his parents and his brother-in-law. He just hoped it wouldn't happen with Kara too.

Check out Love Under Review to read the rest of the story!

ALSO BY BRITNEY M MILLS

The Love, Austen Series
The International Billionaire Series
Sage Creek Small Town Series
Rosemont High Baseball Series
Christmas at Coldwater Creek Series